Addie McCormick

AND THE COMPUTER PIRATE

Leanne Lucas

HARVEST HOUSE PUBLISHERS
Eugene, Oregon 97402

ADDIE McCORMICK AND THE
COMPUTER PIRATE

Copyright © 1994 by Leanne Lucas
Published by Harvest House Publishers
Eugene, Oregon 97402

Library of Congress Cataloging-in-Publication Data

Lucas, Leanne, 1955–
    Addie McCormick and the computer pirate / Leanne C.
Lucas.
        p.   cm. — (Addie McCormick adventures ; 6)
    Summary: While her school is being repaired following
a tornado and she is attending a cooperative home school,
Addie becomes involved in a mystery surrounding the
school's computer software.
    ISBN 1-56507-165-4
    [1. Christian life—Fiction. 2. Schools—Fiction. 3. Mys-
tery and detective stories.] I. Title. II. Series:
Lucas, Leanne, 1955– Addie adventure book ; 6.
PZ7.L96963Ac   1993   93-32203
[Fic]—dc20   CIP
                                                    AC

Printed in the United States of America.

94 95 96 97 98 99 00 — 10 9 8 7 6 5 4 3 2 1

For my son, Joshua,
who is funny.

Contents

Addie
McCormick
AND THE
COMPUTER PIRATE

CHAPTER 1

The Storm

"So what do you want to do, Addie? It's up to you."

Addie bit her lip. "What happens if I run?"

Conor shrugged. "You'll probably get caught. That's what usually happens to me."

"Well, I'm not going back," Addie declared. "I could fight, but someone might get hurt."

"Probably you," Conor murmured.

"Great." Addie sighed. Outside, an ominous roll of thunder filled the silence before she made her decision. "I think I'll hide . . . again." She held her breath, waiting for Nick's response. It came quickly.

"Chicken!" he hissed in her ear, and she poked him in the ribs.

"I'm not chicken," she insisted. "I just think it's better to wait and do nothing sometimes." She punched the number for HIDE into the keyboard and waited for her fate to come up on the screen.

> Your master has passed you by. You are
> safe at the present time.

"I don't believe it!" Nick Brady pushed his chair back from the desk and ran one hand through his blond hair. "Why do you always luck out, Addie?"

Several other children crowded around the desk.

"Did she escape?"

"Addie escaped? Hey, Mrs. Glasgow—"

"No, no, no," Addie interrupted hastily. "I didn't escape."

"She just hid for the third time, and she didn't get caught," Nick informed them.

"She what?" Hillary Jackson squeaked. Hillary was one of Addie's best friends. "I end up wounded or captured whenever I hide."

"All right, everyone," Mrs. Glasgow, the grade school computer instructor, interrupted the friendly banter. "If you're on a computer, you need to save your game. We have some things to talk about before school ends today."

Addie scanned the screen once more and studied the condition of her player, Jolene, a runaway slave from a Georgia plantation. Jolene's nutrition was okay (she just found some berries), her stamina was holding out, but she needed some rest. Maybe next time. Addie punched in the save command, closed the game, and pulled the SHUT DOWN command from the menu. IT IS NOW SAFE TO TURN OFF YOUR COMPUTER flashed on the screen, and Addie flipped the toggle switch on the back of the machine.

She joined her classmates at the long rectangular table in the center of the computer classroom. Nick sat down across from her, and Hillary plopped into the chair on her right.

More thunder rumbled through the open classroom window and Nick frowned. "Spooky weather today," he muttered.

Addie looked out the south windows of the classroom and her heart skipped a beat. Dark thunderheads—big fat ones—sat on the horizon. The air had been hot and heavy all morning with a strange yellow cast to it. Now the wind picked up, and the sky grew considerably darker. Addie shivered.

Mrs. Glasgow glanced out the window, distracted by the weather as well.

"Do you think it'll be a bad storm, Mrs. Glasgow?" Andy Meeker chewed the thumbnail on his right hand while he drummed on the table with his other.

Mrs. Glasgow smiled at the nervous boy. "Probably," she said lightly. "But this is April in Illinois. What else is new?"

The wind outside whistled in agreement, and the teacher clapped her hands sharply. "Let's move on, kids. I've got some great news for you today. First of all, you're going to be seeing a lot more of Conor in the next few weeks."

There was scattered applause, and Conor Davis, a tall, skinny redhead, flashed a broad grin from the back of the room. Conor was a high school sophomore who helped Mrs. Glasgow teach new computer games to all the grade levels once a week.

Mrs. Glasgow continued. "Mr. Mueller, the computer science teacher at the high school, needs guinea pigs to try out some new computer programs for kids. He asked Conor to choose the class he thought would be the easiest to work with, and Conor chose you."

Now there were loud cheers and clapping, and Nick stood up and bowed to his right and to his left. Mrs. Glasgow walked behind his chair and tugged on his hair, hard enough to get him back in his seat.

"Mr. Mueller will be here in just a minute to tell you more about what you'll be doing—"

The door opened on cue, but it was Mr. Stayton, the principal, who walked in with Mrs. Himmel, the sixth-graders' regular teacher. The principal motioned Mrs. Glasgow to the blackboard at the front of the room and turned his back to the children. The three adults spoke in low tones for several moments, then Mr. Stayton hurried from the room.

Mrs. Himmel turned to face her class. Her smile was strained, and she took a deep breath. "We're under a tornado watch," she said briefly. "Nothing has been sighted, but the storm that's coming is pretty bad, with lots of wind. We might have to go to the hallway."

A crack of lightning punctuated her announcement. The thunder that followed was about two seconds away, and Addie could feel the hair rise on her arms. She glanced out the window once more.

The sugar maples that lined the school yard were whipping about in the wind, and Conor and two other boys ran to pull the windows shut. That deadened some of the noise, but the wind moaned eerily through the closed windows.

The classroom door opened once more, and Mr. Mueller strode in. He was a tall, thin man with a big beak of a nose. His coal-black hair had a white streak on one side that gave him a skunk-like appearance. His smile was rare and his manner intense, but his class was a popular one and hard to get into, so no one gave him any trouble.

"Sorry I'm late, Mrs. Glasgow," he said.

Mrs. Glasgow dismissed his apology with a wave of her hand and motioned to the class. "They're ready for you," she said.

Mr. Mueller turned to the group seated at the long table. "Great. Conor and I are eager to have you help us test our new games."

Lightning flashed and thunder rumbled to a crescendo right behind it. A blast of wind made the windows creak, and one near the back of the room banged open. Papers on a shelf nearby swirled to the floor. Conor jumped up to close the window once more, and Mrs. Glasgow gathered the papers and carried them to her desk.

Mr. Mueller waited until the commotion had died down. Then he drew two floppy disks from his shirt pocket and held them up. "There are several math games here and a fairly complex history game. I'm going to load them on your system today." He placed the disks on Mrs. Glasgow's desk near her computer.

"The math games are standard," he continued. "They have their own little twists, but I think you'll find them easy to learn. The history game might be a little tougher. And we've got a surprise for you as well. Right, Conor?"

He smiled briefly and glanced back at the young man. Conor was studying the toes of his shoes, but his face was flushed and he was smiling. He nodded without looking up.

What's going on? Addie wondered to herself. Everyone knew Conor loved computers, but the look on his face was more than just his usual enthusiasm.

"We'll discuss that later," said Mr. Mueller. "I was hoping to show you the games today, but I think we'll have to wait until next week, since class is almost over."

The final bell rang shrilly. "Correction. Class *is* over for today," he amended, speaking loudly to be heard over the noise of chairs scraping.

But the bell stopped in mid-ring, and the class grew still. Then the bell rang again. And stopped. And rang again.

"That's the broken bell," Mrs. Glasgow said loudly, her voice pitched higher than normal. "We're on tornado alert. Everybody out in the hall—now!"

Hillary scooted next to Addie and grabbed her hand. Addie clutched back, and they followed the rest of the class as they filed quickly and silently out the door. Nick remained behind, peering anxiously out the window.

"Nick, get away from the windows and into the hall!" Mrs. Glasgow called from the door.

"Right now!" boomed Mr. Mueller, and Nick made a beeline for the door.

The hallway was unnaturally dark and quiet as children streamed from individual classrooms and sat on the floor in long rows with their backs to the wall. Even from the hall, they could hear the wind reaching a feverish pitch and no one spoke.

Hillary had Addie's hand in an iron grip, but Addie didn't mind. She stared the short distance across the hall and met Nick's eyes.

"I think this would be a good time to pray!" he mouthed.

Addie nodded once in agreement and dropped her head. *Oh, Lord!* she began, but her mind seemed to draw a blank as the wind shrieked wildly. *I can't pray!* she thought in sudden panic. *I can't pray!*

Suddenly she heard her father's voice. *When anxiety was great within me, your consolation brought joy to my soul.*

How did I remember that? she thought in wonderment. *That was in our devotion this morning but . . . Oh, well. Thank You, Lord.* She took a deep, shaky breath. *You're going to take care of us. I know You will. Thank You.*

The wind seemed to calm down some. Nervous chatter and an occasional jittery giggle replaced the silence in the hall.

"No big deal after all," Andy said, but he was interrupted by a strange sound. "What's that?"

They all listened carefully. The sound was coming from the boys' bathroom. The drains were making slurping, sucking noises!

Addie rubbed her ears. They felt funny, like they needed to pop.

Heavy footsteps thundering down the adjacent hall drew everyone's attention. Mr. Stayton—calm, dignified Mr. Stayton—careened around the corner, and there was such alarm in his face, Addie caught her breath.

"Down!" he shouted. "Heads down between your legs! Cover your heads with your hands! It's almost on us!"

Shocked faces stared back at him, and then with one movement, everyone scrunched down and covered their heads.

The silence that followed was the deadliest quiet Addie had ever heard. The air seemed to grow hotter by the second and then the noises began.

First, a chair in the classroom scraped across the floor as if there were still someone in it. Then there was a sharp *pop* and glass shattered to the floor. Then another pop and another until the sound of exploding glass filled the air.

The drains in the bathroom were sucking like crazy now, and the wind changed. It was a sound Addie would never forget for the rest of her life.

Like a monster freight train that was pushing its engine to the limit, the tornado bore down on them with an incredible whining roar. Addie had never heard anything so loud or so frightening, and it only seemed to get worse. The wall at her back shuddered, and she stifled a scream.

Please, Lord—please, Lord—please, Lord—

Addie's heart cried out to God, and her hand groped desperately for Hillary. She locked one arm around her friend and kept the other over her head. Hillary did the same. The two friends clung together as the tornado seemed to suck at them through the walls of the fragile building.

When anxiety was great within me... The sound of her father's voice echoed faintly through the screaming wind.

CHAPTER 2

The Aftermath

The roar of the tornado went on forever. The school building seemed to take on a life of its own as it creaked and cracked in protest under that howling force.

When at last the roar began to subside, Addie ventured a peek out from under her arm. Everyone else had the same idea, and soon the hall was filled with the sounds of children crying quietly at the sight that met their eyes.

The hall was much lighter now—because the roof of the school was gone. Addie looked up through steel beams to see angry clouds boiling overhead.

Lightning flashed and thunder rolled above them. And it was cold—so cold!

"Stay down! Stay down!" Mr. Stayton was on his knees at the far end of the hall, motioning frantically with his hands. "We don't know if it's over yet!"

Every head went down and panicked silence filled the air.

Addie's heart seemed to constrict in her chest. *What else could happen?*

She soon found out. Crashes of thunder followed on the heels of bright lightning, and then the hail began. It came so fast and so hard it was all Addie could do to keep from crying out in pain as the hard, icy drops peppered her back and shoulders.

Lord, PLEASE! Protect us!

Slowly, the thunder and lightning moved into the distance, and the hail softened into slushy rain. Addie was never sure how long they sat scrunched with their heads down in the hallway. The only thing everyone could agree on later was that it seemed like a lifetime.

When she ventured a second look from under her arm, she saw Nick staring at her, dazed. He gave her a shaky smile. Rain—or tears—streaked down his face. She lifted a hand to her own cheek. It was wet, too.

Hillary's face was still buried in her arms, and her shoulders heaved with sobs. Addie slipped an arm around her friend and laid her cheek on Hillary's wet, blonde hair. Mr. Stayton was up now and walking down the hall.

"It's okay. Everything will be all right," he said quietly as he stooped to hug some of the younger children. "We'll take care of you, don't worry." His dark gray hair was plastered to his head by the light rain that was still falling, and his short-sleeve shirt clung to his skin. Addie could see goose bumps on his arms.

Hillary was still crying.

"It's okay, Hillary," Addie murmured. "We're okay. It's all over."

Her friend finally spoke. "But—my mom—" she said and choked back tears. "My mom never . . . goes to the . . . basement in a storm," she said with a hiccup.

Addie didn't answer. Her fear for her own parents seemed to rise up and grab her throat so tightly she couldn't speak. Her father was at work, miles away. He was probably okay. But her mother was home. And home was southwest of the school. And tornadoes usually came out of the southwest . . .

She looked at Nick. He was one of her best friends and her closest neighbor, only a mile down the road. Both their homes had been in the path of the tornado. Nick was blinking rapidly. He covered his eyes with one hand and took several deep breaths. When he finally looked back at Addie, he mouthed four words.

"It's Jesse's nap time."

Addie's stomach flip-flopped. Jesse Kate was Nick's baby sister, and she always napped around two o'clock. Nick's mom usually napped when her daughter did. Had she even heard the storm? Addie closed her eyes and prayed more fervently than she had ever prayed in her life.

Lord, I don't care if everything we own got sucked up by that awful tornado! But please, Lord, PLEASE! Deliver Mom and Dad and Nick's folks and Jesse Kate and Hillary's mom and . . . and everyone else's family. Please, Lord! Please, Lord.

As she finished praying, her spirit grew calm and she sat quietly, her head resting on her knees. Mr. Stayton was talking loudly, trying to be heard over the subdued roar of scared, crying children.

"Everyone stay where you're at. Stay with your teachers. Whitey went to find the bus drivers so we can get the buses and evacuate the building. Until then, teachers, don't let any of your kids go *anywhere*. The safest spot for everyone is right where they're sitting. No one, and I repeat *no one*, should start wandering around."

Whitey, a white-haired, elderly man and one of the school's janitors, stepped through the door frame at the far end of the hall. The glass to the door had shattered, leaving a jagged, gaping hole. He hurried to Mr. Stayton's side, stumbling over outstretched legs and pieces of plaster that Addie hadn't noticed until now.

"No buses," he said with a wheeze and a cough.

"What?"

"Twister took the whole garage. Two of the buses are flattened and one's flipped over in the football field and one's—gone."

Mr. Stayton faltered, but only for a second. "We'll have to wait for emergency vehicles then. They'll be here shortly."

Mr. Mueller joined the two men, and Conor got to his feet as well. The older men seemed to accept him in their group.

"Let's hope that twister lifted before it hit the rest of town," Mr. Mueller said. "Or we'll be on our own out here."

Heritage Grade School was located at the edge of Mt. Pilot, and Addie shuddered at the thought of the damage the tornado might have done through the main part of the village. Maybe *everyone* was stranded, waiting for help to come!

Mr. Mueller gave his shirt pocket an absent-minded pat, then checked it more closely. A look of concern crossed his face and he stepped back and peered into the computer room. Addie followed his gaze.

Most of the computers were face down on the floor, and the table in the center of the room had been tipped on its side. There was glass everywhere, and books and computer catalogs littered the floor, their pages flapping lightly in the wind. Mr. Mueller sighed deeply and turned back to the hall.

Addie prayed Mr. Stayton was right about the emergency vehicles, and he was. Soon they heard the loud *wah—wah—wah* of a siren, then two fire trucks and an ambulance were in the circular drive at the front of the building.

Paramedics came through first, checking for any injured students or teachers. Miraculously, there were none, so the firemen helped students out of the shattered doors at both ends of the building.

Three buses from the Baptist church in Mt. Pilot pulled into the drive next, and all the children were loaded onto these, beginning with the kindergarteners. Many were reluctant to go.

"But my mom won't know where I'm at!" one frightened little girl wailed.

"We're telling all the parents who come to the school that you've been taken to the church. She'll find you there," Mr. Stayton assured her as he picked her up and stood her on the steps to the first bus.

Because they were the oldest at the grade school, Addie's class was the last to board the third bus. Children were crammed four to a seat and a few had to stand. As they pulled away from the devastated building, everyone stared in numbed silence at the destruction.

It looked as if the school had exploded from the inside out. The roof was gone and almost all the windows were shattered. Large pieces of metal were strewn through the school yard, and one big section blocked half of the road.

The drivers from Mt. Pilot Baptist Church slowed down to manuever around the debris, and everyone saw the buses Whitey had described earlier. Two of them looked as if a giant had stepped on them, and the third was upside down in between the goalposts on the football field. The garage that housed the buses was gone. Just gone.

No one spoke, but everyone was thinking the same thing. *What does my house look like?*

The trip through town was quiet, the silence broken only by an occasional muffled sob or hiccup.

There was damage everywhere. Trees were down all over, and one large oak was completely uprooted and resting in the center of the house behind it. Part of the roof was off one gas station, the south wall of the grocery store was gone, and most homes had windows cracked or shattered.

The buses had to drive through an obstacle course of debris in the streets as well. Besides all the branches and overturned garbage cans there were strange things, like a lamp without a shade, a wheelbarrow, a lone cushion from a couch, a huge Oriental rug.

When they reached the Baptist church, there was already a line of cars pulling into the parking lot. There was just enough room for the three buses, and then cars seemed to come from everywhere.

Students poured from the buses, and there were several long minutes of pandemonium as frantic children searched for parents and vice versa. Finally Mr. Stayton managed to get control of the crowd. Someone had found a bullhorn, and the principal stood on the top step of the church and called out instructions.

"Children, if you've found your parents, let your teacher know! Your teacher will take your name down and then you're free to leave. If not, go back to your teacher and stay with him or her. But please! We need to know if you've found a family member. Don't leave without checking with your teacher!"

This common sense advice calmed the crowd down, and soon classes were back together. Teachers were frantically scribbling names on the backs of the Baptist church bulletins from the previous Sunday.

Addie and Nick found Mrs. Himmel. She was writing Hillary's name in the border of her bulletin. Mrs. Jackson had her arm around Hillary, and Hillary was beaming.

"Mom was in the library when the alarm went off," she told Nick and Addie. "The librarian made her get under a table!"

"Addie, have you found your parents?" Mrs. Jackson asked.

Addie shook her head. She had to swallow twice before she could speak. "My mom won't be here for a while. Our car is in the shop, so she'll have to wait for my dad to come home. I know he'll come as soon as he hears about the tornado, but it could be a while."

"Well, why don't you come home with us?" Mrs. Jackson said. "I'm sure Mrs. Himmel can tell your mother—"

"Addie, don't you think my mom would give your mom a ride?" Nick interrupted. "She knows your mom doesn't have a car. I'm sure they'll be together." It was obvious Nick did not want to be left alone, and Mrs. Jackson smiled warmly at the frightened boy.

"You're welcome to come too, Nick," she said.

"Nick! *Nick!*" Suddenly they all heard Mrs. Brady's joyful cry, and Nick pushed his way through to the sidewalk where his mother stood clutching Jesse Kate and waving. Nick embraced them both in a bear hug, and Jesse Kate squealed happily and smacked his head with Mr. Nose, her favorite stuffed toy.

Addie watched the reunion with a shaky smile that bordered on tears. She had never felt so alone in her whole life. She wanted *her* mother!

Then someone had her by the shoulders, and her mother was there. Addie buried her head in the familiar blue sweater and allowed herself to cry for the first time that day. The smell of her mother's perfume mingled with her tears, and they hugged tightly.

Finally Addie sniffed and wiped her nose on the back of her hand. "Where's Dad?" she asked.

"I called him after the tornado went over. He's on his way home." Mrs. McCormick brushed Addie's long black hair from her face and smiled tenderly at her daughter.

"We—we still have a home?" Addie asked tremulously.

"Yes, praise God, we do!" Her mother pulled her close once more, and Addie drew a deep breath of relief and finally relaxed.

Thank You, Lord.

CHAPTER 3

The Cleanup

Twenty minutes later there was another tearful reunion when Addie's father found her, her mother, and the Bradys. They were trying to get back to the Bradys' car, but it was slow going through the debris and the people that clogged the streets of Mt. Pilot.

Mr. McCormick lifted his daughter off her feet in a hug that nearly cracked her ribs. "Thank God you're safe," he murmured. He grabbed Mrs. McCormick by the waist and kissed her cheek.

"When I saw the school, I was pretty frightened," he admitted. "How did they get the elementary kids out?"

Addie frowned. "What do you mean?"

"The new addition on the north end of the school has collapsed," he explained. "Didn't you see it?"

Nick shook his head vehemently. "It was still standing when we left," he protested.

"Well, you got out just in time, then," Mr. McCormick said. "Looks like you guys are in for a little vacation," he told them.

Suddenly Addie clutched her father's hand. "Dad! Miss T. and Amy! We have to get home and—"

Mr. McCormick patted her hand. "I checked on them," he said. He drew in a deep breath. "They're—okay."

The hesitation in his voice made Addie's heart start to pound once more. "What do you mean, Dad? What happened? You don't sound like they're okay!"

"Miss T. and Amy are both fine. The house has a little bit of damage." He paused. "The greenhouse is gone."

Addie and Nick both stared at him. Miss T. was their elderly neighbor, and Amy was her friend and live-in helper. Addie and Nick had met Miss T. last summer, when they were both new to the area. Exciting things had happened in all their lives because of Miss T. and her past history. She was one of their favorite persons. And her greenhouse, empty for many years, had been one of their favorite places to play.

"Of course, the foundation is still there," he went on, "but most of the building is spread through her yard and into the cornfield."

Addie swallowed hard, but she managed to smile. "I don't care," she said softly. "As long as Miss T. and Amy are okay."

"They were beside themselves with worry when they heard about the school on the radio. It had collapsed by then, and Miss T. was convinced you were trapped inside. I said we'd let her know what happened as soon as we could."

"Let's go, then," Mrs. McCormick urged them. "This weather isn't getting a whole lot better. It looks like it could rain again, and these kids are soaked as it is."

The sky was now a depressing steel gray, and a light drizzle began before they reached their car. Mrs. Brady followed Addie's father through the congested streets, and soon they were at the edge of town.

"Dad, stop!" Addie said suddenly. She pointed to a small group of kids trudging down the side of the road. Passing cars splashed rain on the children, and they moved down into the ditch. "That's Conor. He's the high school student that helps out in our computer class."

Conor was carrying a little girl, no more than five years old. A boy who looked to be about thirteen followed him, leading two more girls by the hand.

"It looks like they could use a ride," Mr. McCormick said. He pulled over and tapped lightly on the horn.

Conor looked up and Addie waved. She rolled down her window. "Want a ride, Conor?" she asked.

He shrugged and shook his head. "There's five of us," he said. "We wouldn't all fit in your car."

Mrs. Brady stopped behind the McCormicks, and Nick rolled his window down. "Some of you can ride with us," he called.

One of the younger girls began to sniffle. "Please, Conor," she begged. "I'm cold and I'm tired and I don't wanna walk all the way home. Mama won't care."

Conor nodded. "Okay. Thanks a lot." He helped the three middle children into the backseat with Addie. "Bridget and I will ride with Nick. Just follow Mrs. Brady. It's not far. Thanks again."

Mrs. Brady pulled ahead of them, and a couple of miles down the road they turned north and traveled another quarter mile. They came to a stop in front of a small brick house.

Another little girl, preschool age, came running out the front door. A woman carrying a baby boy was right behind them. The Davis children were out of Addie's car before it came to a stop, and they all crowded around their mother, laughing and hugging and crying.

"Oh, thank God, oh, thank God," Mrs. Davis said over and over as she hugged each of her children several times.

Conor walked back to the Bradys and the McCormicks. "Thank you very much," he said for the third time.

"Is everything okay here?" Mr. McCormick asked. "Do you need anything before we go?"

Mrs. Davis heard the question and she laughed. "I don't need a thing now that I know my children are safe," she said. "We've got a tree on our back porch," she added, "but I've called my husband, and he'll be here directly. We'll manage. God bless you for bringing my children home."

They backed out of the Davises' drive. Finally Mrs. McCormick spoke. "Seven children," she said softly.

"In that dinky little house," Addie said.

"We'll stop by tomorrow and see how they're doing," Mr. McCormick added firmly.

By now Addie was very cold and her head hurt. They stopped by Miss T.'s only long enough to assure the elderly woman the two children were all right. Her yard was a mess, and Mr. McCormick promised her they would be by the next day to help clean up the debris.

"We're sure going to be busy tomorrow, aren't we?" Addie asked in a tired voice.

"I have a feeling we're going to be busy for quite a while," Mr. McCormick said grimly.

* * *

Although the McCormicks' home and the Bradys' home had been spared any real damage, many of their friends and neighbors had not been as fortunate. Almost everyone they knew needed help of some kind.

Addie, Nick, and their fathers began at Miss T.'s. It was hard work picking up the old lumber and plaster that had once been the greenhouse. And there was glass everywhere. The south wall had been all windows. Addie remembered the day she and Nick helped Miss T. clean the greenhouse. She had the job of washing the windows. She'd said then she never wanted to see another window.

Addie reminded Nick of that day. "I wish those windows were still here to clean," she said.

He nodded. "It'd be a lot easier washing them than it is picking them out of this grass," he said. It was awkward work because Miss T. made them wear thick leather gloves and boots so they wouldn't get cut.

Mr. McCormick and Mr. Brady were doing the heavy work, dragging pieces of siding and framework to the drive, where they stacked them in big piles. They had tried to hire a truck to haul the garbage away, but there wasn't one to be found in a thirty-mile radius. They were all in Mt. Pilot, hauling away *that* garbage.

Late in the afternoon the two men, Addie, and Nick hopped in the Bradys' station wagon and drove to Conor Davis's home. Conor and his father were busy with saws, cutting up the tree that had flattened their back porch.

After Conor introduced everyone, Mr. McCormick spoke bluntly. "I'm sure there are things you need," he said. "What can we do to help?"

Mr. Davis was a quiet-spoken man. "Well, we're needing food, mostly. When the tree went down, it took our light pole with it, so we've had no electricity for a day. The kids have eaten dry cereal and fruit, but they could use a hot meal."

"It's done," Mr. McCormick said with a grin. "We'll take your wife and the younger kids back with us to our house. Why don't you and Conor and—" he hesitated as he nodded at the younger boy.

"Liam," the boy said shyly.

"You and Conor and Liam finish up here and come over to our house in about an hour. We'll have supper waiting for you."

Mr. Davis smiled gratefully. "Thank you, sir. We'll enjoy that."

It was a tight fit with Mrs. Davis and the five youngest Davises in the Bradys' station wagon, but it was a fun trip. When Mr. Brady dropped them all off at the McCormicks' house, Addie had met Anna, Mary, and Bridget Davis. Kerry was the preschooler and Sean was the baby.

When all the Davises filed into the McCormick kitchen, Addie noticed a very surprised look on her mom's face. But Mrs. McCormick recovered almost immediately and went directly to the freezer in the garage. She pulled out three big tubs of frozen pork barbecue, three packages of hamburger buns, and a bag of frozen corn.

An hour later, there was a large sheet spread over the floor in the dining room, and Davises were everywhere, eating sandwiches and corn off paper plates. It was a noisy, happy meal, and Addie enjoyed it thoroughly. Even Mrs. McCormick seemed to be having a good time.

When most of the food was gone, Addie sat down next to Conor. Sean was snuggled in his lap, almost asleep.

"I guess you won't be teaching us those new computer games for a while," she said.

Conor frowned. "Guess not," he muttered.

"Maybe next year," Addie said, trying to cheer him up.

Conor only shrugged.

"What was the surprise Mr. Mueller was talking about?" Addie asked the older boy.

Conor took a deep breath and a smile tugged at the corners of his mouth. "We had some . . . special programs we wanted to show you," he said. "Mr. Mueller teaches a class on computer programming, and we've been doing some pretty cool stuff."

Then his expression changed. "I hope the work we've done this year isn't ruined," he said in a dejected voice. "The whole system probably crashed when the tornado hit the high school."

The idea seemed to depress him, so Addie hurried to change the subject. "You know how to write your own computer programs?"

Conor nodded, embarrassed but pleased at the admiration in Addie's voice. "It's fun. Mr. Mueller says I'm a natural at it."

"That's great, Conor," Addie told him. "My dad says anyone who knows their way around computers will get the really good jobs in the future."

Conor nodded firmly. "That's what I'm going to do. Be a computer programmer—or something like that. I like to draw, too. Maybe I'll go into computer graphics." He hesitated. "There are men who've made *millions* writing computer software. That's what I'm going to do."

He said the last statement with such fierceness, Addie was surprised.

"Money isn't everything," she offered timidly.

Conor's expression softened, and he glanced fondly at the baby asleep in his lap. "I know. But it helps. It helps *a lot*. And there's going to be a day when I've got enough of it to buy everything I want. Everything my family wants. Not just what we need. And I'll do whatever I have to do to get it."

He glared at Addie so defiantly she lowered her eyes. *I'd hate to be the person who gets in his way*, she thought to herself.

CHAPTER 4

What About School?

The next day was Sunday, and the church was crowded. Although several of the building's south windows had been broken and were now boarded up, there was no other damage. Addie sat next to her parents and listened to the prayer requests and praises of their friends and neighbors.

"I thank God my family is safe," Gordon Johnson said. He choked back tears, and the rest of the congregation waited patiently until he could speak once more. Gordon's home had been destroyed, and his wife and baby had been trapped in their basement under the rubble for more than an hour before emergency crews were able to get them out.

"We're living with my sister right now, and the Lord's provided everything we need. You've all been so generous. I don't think the baby will run out of diapers for a year!"

Everyone laughed and Gordon continued. "We're going to rebuild, although I'm not sure when. It's going to be tough financially for a while. But I'm not complaining. When I watched them pull Kathy and the baby out of that mess Friday afternoon, I thanked God for reminding me what the important things are in life. And I know we'll get back on our feet. He'll take care of us."

Mrs. Dodson, one of the cooks at Heritage, had another praise. "Five minutes after the buses left to take the children to the church, firemen were putting yellow tape all around the building to warn people of the danger there. The north addition collapsed before they were finished! It was a miracle no one was left inside. I thank God for protecting us all!"

And so it went, for the better part of an hour.

"Praise the Lord Grandma had her hearing aid in and heard the siren!"

"I'm glad my dog Saphire was inside when the tornado hit."

"Thank God for neighbors with big freezers full of food!"

"I'm grateful that tornado flipped over our old '84 Ford instead of our brand-new van!"

During the break that followed the message, Addie, Hillary, Nick, and Andy slipped down to the basement to talk.

"Conor Davis told me about the surprise Mr. Mueller had planned for our computer class," Addie informed them. "They were going to show us some programs they wrote in their computer programming class."

Nick was impressed. "That takes brains. Brian could do that. He took classes on computer programming at Kids College last semester."

Brian Dennison was a good friend of Nick's. He had spent the previous semester with the Bradys while his father traveled to Japan to set up headquarters for his corporation. Brian had joined his father in Japan right before Christmas.

"Brian and Conor would have gotten along great," Hillary said.

"Say, Addie," Nick said, "did Conor have a copy of those programs? He could show them to us on Brian's computer. It's compatible with the school's." Brian had left his computer with Nick for safekeeping since his father already had a computer in Japan.

Addie shook her head. "Conor is pretty sure everything was destroyed in the tornado. He was really upset at the idea of losing all the work he'd done. I think we should pray and ask God to—to find those programs."

Andy was doubtful. "I don't know much about computers, Addie, but once a program's crashed, it's gone. My mom was doing research for her thesis one night when a storm hit and the power went out. It wiped out all her work."

"It doesn't hurt to pray," Addie insisted. "God's bigger than any computer." No one wanted to argue with that, but there were no rousing "Amens" either, so Addie let it drop.

Hillary brought up a more pressing subject. "Does anyone know what we're going to do about school?"

"I think the best idea is to forget school for the rest of the year," Nick said solemnly. His suggestion was met with hoots of laughter.

"Really," he protested. "We only have a few weeks left—"

"Almost eight," Addie interrupted.

"And there will be so much work to do to clean up the town, we should just consider the rest of the year like—like a work program, the way they do in high school," he finished.

"No such luck," Andy said. "I'm sure they'll figure out some way to get us back in school."

Andy was right. Although classes were canceled the next week and businesses shut down so everyone could help in the massive cleanup, the superintendent scheduled a meeting for all parents on Wednesday night.

Addie and Nick babysat Jesse Kate at Nick's house while their parents attended the meeting. When they returned, Mrs. Brady fixed coffee and Mr. Brady called the two children into the kitchen.

"So what's the word?" Nick asked eagerly. "Is school over for the year?"

Mr. Brady rapped his son lightly on the head with a rolled-up paper. "How many times do I have to tell you, the school can't just write off the last two months of classes!"

"Okay, okay," Nick muttered.

Mr. Brady continued, "You're scheduled to go back to school on Monday."

"What?" Nick exclaimed.

"Where?" Addie asked.

Mr. Brady sighed. "You'll be bused to Marshall City for the rest of the year."

"That's an hour away," Nick complained.

"Only forty-five minutes," his mother said.

"They're sending all of us to Marshall City?" Addie asked.

Mr. McCormick shook his head. "No. MC can only handle about half of Mt. Pilot's students, so the other half will be bused to Loman."

"That's an hour away in the other direction!" Nick exclaimed.

"Only forty-five minutes," his mother said.

"Okay," Nick said impatiently. "Only forty-five minutes. It still means we'll all spend an hour-and-a-half on the bus every day."

"Where's Hillary going?" Addie wanted to know.

"And Andy?" Nick asked.

"They're going to Loman," Mr. McCormick said.

Addie and Nick were silent. Finally Nick spoke. "We won't know anyone at Marshall City," he grumbled.

"We'll have some of our classmates," Addie said. "And we'll know each other."

Mr. McCormick cleared his throat and consulted a paper he pulled from his back pocket. "That's the other thing," he said. "They have two sixth-grade classes at MC. You won't be together."

"Dad!" Addie couldn't keep the whine out of her voice. "You mean I've got to start all over with new friends—again?!"

"We know it's going to be tough, sweetie," Mrs. McCormick said.

"It's going to be terrible," Addie snapped.

Her father gave her a stern look. "It's not your mother's fault," he said. "And it's only for two months."

"Sorry, Mom," Addie murmured.

Mrs. McCormick gave her daughter a hug. "I wish there were some other way, Addie. But there's not. We'll just have to make this work."

"And pray for summer to come," Nick muttered.

* * *

Nick stopped by the McCormicks' early Thursday morning to show Addie a letter he'd just received from Brian.

Addie read through the letter quickly, then went back and picked out bits and pieces. "Brian's on a baseball team and he's got the highest batting average . . . he loves sushi . . ."

"What's sushi?" Nick asked.

"Raw fish," Addie told him.

"That's gross!" Nick shuddered.

"His dad hired a tutor to help him learn Japanese," she continued.

"I wish we could hire a tutor," Nick interrupted. "Then we could stay home and go to school."

"Yeah, right," Addie scoffed. "Tutors are expensive."

"How expensive?"

"Too expensive on my dad's salary," Addie said.

"Yeah, mine too, probably," Nick agreed.

Suddenly Addie sat up straight and stared at Nick.

"What?" Nick asked. "What'd I say?"

"That part about staying home to go to school," Addie said. "Have you ever met Kate and Kelly . . . oh, I can't remember their last name. They just moved here in January. They visited our church once or twice."

Nick shook his head. "What about 'em?"

"Their mom teaches them at home."

Nick frowned. "Is that . . . legal?"

"Sure it's legal," Addie said. "At least, I think it is. I mean, I'm sure it is. I don't think they'd go around breaking the law."

Nick wrinkled his nose. "Isn't that kind of weird? I mean, do you really think you'd like your mom to be your teacher?"

Addie shrugged. "I think I'd like it better than going to another new school."

"That's true," Nick agreed. "I don't think my mom would go for it, though. She's got her hands full taking care of Jess."

"Maybe they could work together," Addie said. "Or maybe Kate and Kelly's mom would help us. Joyce. That's her name. She's real nice. And she knows all about teaching sixth grade because Kate is in eighth. That means they got through sixth okay."

Nick still looked doubtful. "I don't know, Addie."

"It can't hurt to ask," Addie exclaimed. "All they can say is no. We'd be no worse off than we are now."

Nick grinned. "Okay. Let's do it."

They ran to the kitchen, where Mrs. McCormick was just taking a batch of chocolate chip cookies out of the oven.

"Let me help you, Mom," Addie said. She took two pot holders and set them on the table so Mrs. McCormick could set the hot cookie sheet down. "Nick and I want to talk to you."

Mrs. McCormick eyed the children suspiciously. "I've seen that look on your faces before. What are you two cooking up now?"

Nick grinned and pulled out a chair at the table. "Have a seat, Mrs. McCormick," he said. "Have we got a deal for you!"

CHAPTER 5

School . . .
Home . . . Homeschool?

To Addie's surprise, Mrs. McCormick listened to their impromptu presentation on the benefits of being schooled at home. She didn't interrupt them or scoff at the idea. In fact, she didn't say anything at all. When they were finished, the kitchen was silent.

Finally Addie spoke. "You always said you wished we could spend more time together, Mom. Well, this is your big chance."

Mrs. McCormick laughed. "Put my money where my mouth is, huh?"

Addie grinned. "So to speak."

"Well, to be honest with you, I kind of like the idea," Mrs. McCormick said. "I admire Joyce McLane. She makes homeschooling look very attractive. And her girls are certainly great kids."

"You really might do this?" Nick looked from Addie to Mrs. McCormick and back to Addie. "I don't believe it!"

"Wasn't that the idea?" Mrs. McCormick laughed. "Why did you even bother to ask if you didn't think there was a chance I'd consider it?"

"I was just humoring Addie," Nick grinned.

Addie stuck her tongue out at him. "Very funny."

Nick sighed. "This is just great. You get to stay home, and I'll be going to Marshall City by myself. My mom will never go for it."

"I haven't said *I'm* going to do it for sure," Mrs. McCormick said hastily. "This is not a decision to make on the spur of the moment. I'll have to talk with your dad about it, and we'll have to give it some prayer."

She emptied the last cookie sheet and stuck the pan in the dishwater. It sizzled briefly and she dropped the spatula in the water next to it. "Still, it has possibilities. We might even—" But she shook her head and grew quiet.

"What, Mom? We might even what?" Addie asked eagerly.

"Nothing. I have to talk with your father." Mrs. McCormick's tone was final, so Addie didn't try to coax any more out of her.

Instead, she motioned to Nick, and they slipped out the back door and sat under the big sugar maple in the front yard.

"Wouldn't it be great if she decided to teach you, too?" she said to Nick.

Nick's face brightened considerably, but then he frowned. "She can't do that, can she? I mean, she's not my mom."

"Joyce McLane teaches the Byers' little boy in the morning. He's only five. Mrs. Byers didn't want to send him to kindergarten yet, so Joyce is working with him on some preschool stuff," Addie said.

"Yeah, but that's preschool. Nobody cares about that. This is sixth grade. I wouldn't want to get your mom arrested or anything." Nick looked worried. "I wouldn't want my folks to get arrested either."

Addie laughed. "Nobody's going to get arrested. If it was illegal, my mom wouldn't even consider it. Just think, Nick. We might be homeschooled!"

Mrs. McCormick wasted little time. That evening, Addie heard her parents talking late into the night. Bits and pieces of their conversation drifted up the stairs, and Addie tried hard to stay awake to listen.

"What about curriculum . . . ?"

"Will she miss her friends too much . . . ?"

"What do you think the school will say . . . ?"

The next morning Mrs. McCormick sent Addie down to the Bradys'. She and Nick watched Jesse Kate once more while Mrs. Brady spent the morning at Addie's house, drinking coffee and talking.

Still, no one would tell Addie and Nick anything until that evening. The Bradys came to the McCormicks house for supper, and the children could barely contain their curiosity until Mrs. McCormick cleared the table for dessert.

Mr. McCormick grinned at the anxious children. "What's your problem, anyway?"

"Dad!" Addie practically shouted. "Will someone please tell us what's going on?"

He laughed and tugged her long, black braid. "Think Mom can handle the two of you for the next couple of months?" he asked.

"Yes!" Nick shouted, and Addie clapped her hands gleefully.

"Hang on," Mr. McCormick laughed. "We still have some things to check out. But your mom and I prayed about this last night, and we both felt confident it was something the Lord wanted us to do."

"So I called Joyce McLane this morning," Mrs. McCormick said. "She's got curriculum we can use. It doesn't match up exactly with what you've been using at the public school, but it will be all right for the next few weeks."

"And you'll have to write out most of your work," Mr. McCormick warned them. "We won't have the workbooks you're used to. You'll have to share a lot of books."

"Gwen will teach you all the academic subjects," Mrs. Brady added. "I'll take you in the afternoons two or three times a week for art projects. That was my major in college. And it's something we can include Jesse Kate in if she wakes up from her nap. She can make a mess without being too much of a distraction."

"Where will we have class?" Addie asked.

"In our spare room," Mr. McCormick said. "This is a great chance to get that cleaned out. I'll set up a big table for you and Nick and a desk for your mom."

Addie snapped her fingers. "We could bring Brian's computer here, too! Do you think Brian would mind?" she asked Nick.

"Of course not. We don't get much of a chance to use it at Miss T.'s."

Miss T. had a room the children had cleaned and decorated and used for a club whenever they visited her. Brian's computer was set up there so Jesse Kate couldn't get to it.

"When do we start?" Addie asked.

"Sometime next week," Mrs. McCormick answered. "I don't think I can get everything ready by Monday. Maybe Tuesday or Wednesday."

"So we get a couple extra days of vacation," Nick grinned.

Mr. McCormick grinned back. "Just enough time to clean out that spare room."

Even the prospect of two days of cleaning couldn't dampen the children's spirits. When they arrived at church Sunday they were bursting with the news. Hillary and Andy were excited for their friends, but neither of them was eager to go to their new school.

"I wish my mom would teach me at home," Hillary said wistfully.

Addie said nothing, but when the children went to the sanctuary for the main service, she held a whispered conversation with her parents.

Mr. McCormick was doubtful, but Mrs. McCormick seemed undaunted. "John, I taught thirty fifth-graders every year for eight years before Addie was born," she said. "I think I can handle three or four sixth-graders."

After much discussion, it was decided that the Jacksons and the Meekers would bring Hillary and Andy to the McCormicks to finish the school year.

The four children spent Sunday and Monday cleaning out the spare room at Addie's house and scrounging through attics and basements for tables, chairs, lamps, bulletin boards, and assorted odds and ends to furnish the new "classroom." By Monday night there was a dark blue carpet remnant on the floor, new blue curtains at the windows, a chalkboard on one wall, and two large bulletin boards on another.

Mrs. McCormick had a "desk" at the front of the room (a long door set on two short file cabinets), and the children had a large round table with four wicker chairs. They also had a set of shelves (one shelf per person), two bean bag chairs, and a rocker for silent reading time. Brian's computer occupied a place of honor under the window on the only real desk with drawers. When they were finished, the children surveyed their work with pride.

"This is going to be great!" Nick exclaimed.

Addie hugged her mom tightly. "Thanks, Mom," she whispered. "I'll never forget this."

The next day, the four children greeted one another with excited chatter. Was this really going to work? Mrs. McCormick smiled at their nervous anticipation.

"We're going to start school in a way you've never done before," she said. "We'll open with prayer and read a passage from our Bibles before we begin studying. Does anyone have any special prayer requests?"

There was a somewhat shocked silence, then Andy raised his hand timidly. "My mom's not feeling very good today. Could we pray for her?"

Mrs. McCormick nodded. "Nick?"

"Brian needs help with his schoolwork. He's having a tough time learning Japanese."

"Okay. Anything else? Let's pray." Mrs. McCormick prayed for their new school and the requests that had been made. Then they read several psalms and a chapter from Proverbs. When they were finished, everyone was relaxed and ready to begin.

The first day of "homeschool" flew by, with only a few hitches. Because they were short on books, Addie and Hillary worked on math and science while Nick and Andy did language arts and health. After break, they switched books and worked until noon. When lunch was finished, they all worked on history and geography. Then Mrs. Brady came to take them to Nick's house, and they began work on a diorama of a Bible-time village.

It was a full day, and Addie was tired when she got home around three o'clock. Her mother greeted her with a smile.

"So. What did you think?"

Addie grinned. "I think I worked harder today than I have all year!" she exclaimed. "But I loved it."

"Good," her mother said. "I enjoyed it, too. Say, do you want to ride to town with me? I have to pick up some groceries for supper. I've been so busy getting ready for school, I forgot to go shopping Saturday."

At the grocery store in Mt. Pilot, Addie and her mom were in the frozen food section when they heard someone call their names. It was Mrs. Davis with Conor and Liam. Each of them was pushing a grocery cart, and the carts were full.

"Hello, Gwen," Mrs. Davis said warmly. "I've been meaning to call you. How have you been?"

"Well, pretty busy," Mrs. McCormick laughed and told the Davises about their newest venture.

Mrs. Davis was impressed. "I think it would be such a wonderful opportunity to learn with your children."

Conor spoke wistfully. "You have your own computer?"

Addie nodded. "Did you get a chance to check the system at the high school to see if your programs were wiped out?"

Conor shook his head. "They won't let students in the building," he said. "It's too dangerous."

"Are you doing any programming at Marshall City?" Addie asked.

"No," Conor said shortly. "My computer science class at MC is so crowded I haven't even had a chance to get on the computer yet."

"Would you like to work on our computer?" Mrs. McCormick asked suddenly.

Conor's face lit up, but his mother spoke before he had a chance. "That's very kind of you, but I can't let Conor impose on you like that."

"Oh, it wouldn't be an imposition," Mrs. McCormick insisted. "Addie's told me how much he helped in her computer class at Heritage. I thought maybe we could work something out. I'm pretty illiterate when it comes to computers. We have lots of programs, but I don't know how to use any of them. Conor could come by after school and spend some time teaching me the ropes. The rest of the time he'd be free to use the computer himself."

Mrs. Davis looked doubtful, but the longing in Conor's face was too much for her to resist. "Well, if you think he could be a help to you, I guess I'd be willing to let him try it."

Arrangements were made for Conor to come out the following day. When the two families parted, Conor was almost floating down the aisle of the grocery store.

"Thanks, Mom," Addie said when they were out of earshot. "I don't think you know how important—"

"Gwen."

A sharp, shrill voice interrupted Addie, and she and her mother turned to see Mrs. Kreiling, a woman from their church, regarding them with a frown.

"I hear you're teaching—at home."

"Yes, I am," Mrs. McCormick said. "We just started today."

"Well. I'm sure that's none of my business. I suppose you think you're doing what's best."

Addie's mother didn't answer. She only nodded and smiled, but Addie noticed her smile was strained.

"Well. Be that as it may," Mrs. Kreiling continued, "I couldn't help but hear your conversation with that family."

Mrs. McCormick's smile faded, and she remained silent.

"I think you need to know—for your own good, mind you—that's the Davis family. They've got more children than you can count. And none of them can be trusted. Especially that oldest boy. What's his name? Conor? I wouldn't want him around my children. He's nothing but trouble."

CHAPTER 6

Ugly Rumors

In less than a minute, Mrs. Kreiling accused Conor of everything from spray-painting graffiti on the bridge at the overpass to looting the local mini-mall after the tornado.

"Everyone knows he and some other boys cleaned out Blacker's Jewelry Store Saturday afternoon. Why, I even heard—"

"Everyone *doesn't* know that." Mrs. McCormick interrupted the gossipy woman. "I haven't heard Mr. Blacker making any accusations. I'm not about to make a judgment based on hearsay."

"Well, I'd never do that," Mrs. Kreiling said

indignantly. "Caroline Thomas told me her husband was talking to a man who *saw* them. And do you know, the Davises' baby isn't hardly a year old and Caroline told me she thinks that woman is pregnant *again*."

Mrs. McCormick smiled tightly. "I'll invite their family to church Sunday. You can ask Mrs. Davis yourself."

Mrs. Kreiling was so shocked she stuttered and then shut her mouth with a snap. Addie's mother said a quick goodbye and pushed her cart to the checkout line. Addie knew they weren't finished shopping, but she said nothing. Mrs. McCormick paid for her groceries, and Addie bagged them and carried them to the car.

It was often difficult for Addie to tell when her mother was angry, but Mrs. McCormick always gave herself away if she was driving. She would stomp on the clutch, ram the stick shift into the next gear, and then gun the engine. Stomp, ram, vrooom! Stomp, ram, vroom! By the time she reached fifth gear, she was usually calmed down, but the three gears before that were always breathtaking.

Addie waited until they were in fifth gear before she ventured a question. "Do you think Mrs. Kreiling knows the Davises very well?"

"She doesn't know them at all," Mrs. McCormick snapped. Then she took a deep breath and glanced at her daughter. "Sorry, hon."

Addie grinned. "That's okay. She made me mad, too." They rode in silence for several blocks. Then Addie asked, "Why do you suppose she suspects Conor of doing all those things?"

Her mother shrugged. "Maybe Conor has been in a little trouble before. I don't know. It only takes one time for a kid to get a reputation. That's why the Bible tells us to avoid even the *appearance* of evil. That way you don't give the Mrs. Kreilings of the world any fuel for their fire."

Addie sighed. "I know Conor hates being poor," she said.

Her mother gave her a curious glance. "How do you know that?"

"Just some things he said the night they came over for supper."

Her mother patted her hand. "Well, let's just forget that whole scene with Mrs. Kreiling, shall we? We certainly aren't doing Conor any favors if we let gossip affect the way we think about him."

"Are you really going to invite the Davises to church?" Addie asked.

Mrs. McCormick burst out laughing. "I am now," she said.

When they arrived home, Mr. McCormick was frying potatoes for supper. He kissed his wife lightly and hugged Addie. "Thought I'd make myself useful until you got home."

Addie loved her father's fried potatoes. He always used real butter and lots of salt and pepper. Her mother said she could feel her arteries clogging up with cholesterol whenever she ate them, but Addie didn't worry about it. They tasted wonderful.

"I had a very productive afternoon," Mr. McCormick said as he tested his potatoes, then added more salt. "I met the high school computer science teacher. Jim Mueller. He's helping me organize the family-to-family committees. We're going to put the list on computer." Addie's father was pairing up families that could be of help to one another after the tornado.

"I know him," Addie said. She told her parents about his appearance in her class on the day of the tornado. "He seems like a nice guy," she concluded.

Her father nodded. "He is. Very interesting, too, and intelligent. I guess teaching doesn't pay enough to support his family, so he moonlights for a software company in Chicago. Does some R&D."

"What's R&D?" Addie asked.

"Research and development," he told her. "When he found out we were homeschooling, he offered to help with lesson plans for a mini-computer class for the four of you."

"That would be wonderful!" Mrs. McCormick exclaimed. "Conor Davis is going to come out and help me learn the different programs we have. If Mr. Mueller helps me organize them into some sort of curriculum for the kids, I'll be all set."

"Conor is coming here?" Mr. McCormick asked.

Addie's mom told her husband about the arrangement they made with Conor at the grocery store that afternoon. She made no mention of their conversation with Mrs. Kreiling.

Mr. McCormick listened quietly. When she was finished, he said nothing.

"Is that all right?" she asked hesitantly.

He smiled and shrugged. "Sure, I guess so."

"John, what's the matter?"

Addie tried to shrink into a corner of the kitchen with the hope that her dad would forget she was there and continue the conversation. No such luck.

Mr. McCormick glanced at his daughter and back at his wife.

"I don't think Addie will repeat anything you say," Mrs. McCormick said dryly. "She's already heard an earful about Conor and his family today. Nothing you can say will shock her too much."

Mr. McCormick raised one eyebrow. "Oh, yeah? Jim—Mr. Mueller—had some pretty strong opinions about the family, too. But he really likes the boy. I guess Conor's quite a computer genius. But he needs some . . . supervision. So Jim took him under his wing this year."

"Lots of people have strong opinions about that family," said Mrs. McCormick. She gave her husband a condensed version of their conversation with Mrs. Kreiling. Mr. McCormick just shook his head as his wife told him about the unkind accusations.

"I sure hope she's wrong," he said when his wife finished. "I'"m going to go on the assumption that she *is* wrong, unless Conor gives us reason to believe otherwise." He hesitated. "Just . . . keep an eye on him," he said quietly.

Addie's heart sank. What if there were some truth to those ugly rumors? She hoped for Conor's sake that's all they were—ugly rumors.

The second day of homeschool passed as quickly as the first. When the other children learned Conor was coming out to work on the computer after school, no one wanted to go home at the end of the day. But Mrs. Jackson arrived at three-thirty to pick up Hillary and Andy, so they bid their friends a reluctant farewell.

"See you tomorrow!" Hillary called from the car window.

Addie waved until they were out of sight. Nick sat on his ten-speed, ready to ride the mile to his house.

"So Conor's going to teach your mom how to use the computer."

Addie nodded.

"Conor won't know what to do when he has a computer all to himself," Nick grinned. "He'll never want to go home! 'Course, I wouldn't either, if I were him." He paused. "Can you believe all the kids they've got?"

"So?" Addie snapped.

"What do you mean, so? Nobody has seven kids anymore!"

"I think it would be fun to have so many brothers and sisters," Addie said.

"No you wouldn't," Nick scoffed. "You'd never have any privacy. And all your clothes would be hand-me-downs. You'd never get to buy anything new. I think it would be a bummer being that poor."

"There are more important things than money!" Addie stormed. She picked a rock out of the driveway and hurled it across the road.

"Tell that to the people that don't have any," Nick said. He wrinkled his nose at Addie. "What's your problem? You're sure a grouch all of a sudden. I'm going home. Tell Conor hi for me."

He rode off without a backward glance, and Addie slumped to the grass and leaned back against the maple tree in their front yard. She stayed there until the Davises pulled in about twenty minutes later.

Conor jumped out of the front seat before the car came to a stop. Mrs. Davis rolled down her window. "I'll be back at six," she said with a smile.

"See ya, Ma," Conor waved. He and Addie walked in the back door and Addie showed him down the hall to the classroom. Conor was properly impressed with their miniature school and anxious to get to the computer.

For the next hour the young boy worked with Mrs. McCormick, showing her the ins and outs of various programs. She learned how to personalize math games and spelling lists for each student, how to set up contests between two players and print out scoresheets. Addie sat in a chair next to them and listened to everything.

Finally, Mrs. McCormick pushed her chair away from the desk and closed her eyes. "That's enough for today, Conor. If you load any more information into my 'computer' I think *I'm* going to crash!"

Conor grinned and glanced at his watch. "It is almost five o'clock," he said. "I lose track of time when I'm on a computer."

"Well, the next hour is yours," Mrs. McCormick smiled. Then her smile faded and Addie followed her glance.

The watch Conor wore was one of the fanciest Addie had ever seen. It had a miniature calculator on it, and there were all kinds of buttons and knobs on both sides. It had a heavy, gold-plated band that sparkled in the sunlight. It looked very expensive.

. . . cleaned out Blacker's Jewelry Store . . .

Addie couldn't stop the ugly words from racing through her mind. She squeezed her eyes shut and shook her head.

Mrs. McCormick stood up abruptly and patted Conor's shoulder. "Enjoy yourself," she said. "Come on, Addie. Let's fix supper."

Addie followed her mother out of the room with a heavy heart.

CHAPTER 7

Rumors ... or Truth?

Addie didn't talk much at supper. When she was finished, she cleared the table quickly and loaded the dishwasher. Then she excused herself and spent the rest of the night in her room, trying to read. But she couldn't concentrate so she got ready for bed, then went downstairs to tell her parents good night.

Mrs. McCormick patted the sofa next to her, and Addie sat down. Her mother began braiding Addie's long black hair, and Addie felt herself relax. She loved it when her mother fixed her hair.

"Addie," her mom said, "I know you're worried about Conor."

Addie nodded and voiced the nagging doubts she'd had all night. "How could he afford that beautiful watch, Mom?"

Her mother sighed. "I don't know, honey. But things aren't always what they seem. Let's not judge Conor too hastily, okay?"

"Okay."

Mrs. McCormick took the rubber band from the evening paper and secured Addie's braid. Then she hugged her daughter tightly. "We'll just keep him in our prayers."

Addie nodded and closed her eyes. Mrs. McCormick prayed softly, thanking the Lord for His blessing on their homeschool. Then she prayed for wisdom in their relationship with Conor and his family. Mr. McCormick joined his wife and daughter before the prayer was over. When they were finished, Addie gave both her parents a kiss and a hug and went to bed. She fell asleep quickly and slept soundly.

The next day seemed to pass a little slower as the children settled into a routine and adjusted to their new situation. Nick was goofing off more than usual, and Mrs. McCormick had to admonish him several times. When she threatened to make him work through the morning break, he settled down quickly.

"Aren't you glad there's only one of me?" he asked Mrs. McCormick with an ornery grin as the four children snacked on granola bars and apple juice.

Mrs. McCormick grinned back. "I'll remember to

add that to my list of blessings," she said with a wink.

Nick pretended to dribble his granola bar wrapping then tossed it into the garbage with an over-the-head hook shot.

"Two points!" he whooped. "Just imagine," he continued, "what it would be like with seven kids. You'd go crazy!"

"My aunt and uncle have six kids," Andy said. "My mom gets real nervous whenever they come to visit. The older kids are supposed to watch the younger ones, but they never do. The baby always ends up eating something he shouldn't, and the twins take turns jumping off my bunk bed. Mom says she considers it a good visit if they all leave our house alive."

Andy's droll description of his cousins had everyone laughing, even Mrs. McCormick.

"I imagine there's always something going on in a big family," she agreed.

"The Davises have seven kids," Hillary said. "We saw the whole family at a restaurant once. They needed two tables."

"My grandma says there's always a troublemaker in a family that big," Andy said. "I wonder who the troublemaker is in Conor's family?"

"Probably Conor," Nick laughed.

Addie pushed her chair back from the table with a loud scrape. "There's a troublemaker in every family, large or small," she said and glared at Nick.

"*Moi?*" Nick said in a shocked voice.

Andy and Hillary laughed, but Addie refused to join in and their laughter faded.

"Can't you take a joke, Addie?" Nick complained. "Can't you—"

"Okay, okay," Mrs. McCormick interrupted the heated exchange and gave her daughter a warning look. "Let's just drop it, all right? You've only got a few minutes left in your break. Don't spend it fighting."

There was an awkward silence. Addie scooted her chair back to the table and opened the book she'd been reading. Hillary, Andy, and Nick talked quietly for a few more minutes, then class resumed.

There was no further mention of Conor or his family. By lunchtime, Addie and Nick came to an unspoken truce and everyone relaxed. The afternoon passed quickly. This time Mrs. Meeker came to pick up Hillary and Andy. Nick and Addie watched their friends leave.

"Want to ride down to the creek, maybe over to see Miss T. and Amy?" Nick's question was casual, but Addie knew it was his way of apologizing. She hated to refuse, but she shook her head.

"Conor is coming back this afternoon. I'd like to be here when he comes. I really want to learn some of those computer games Brian left, and Mom says she can't remember everything herself."

Nick didn't answer, so Addie plunged into her own apology.

"Look, Nick, I'm sorry I about this morning."

Nick shrugged. "S'okay," he said briefly.

But Addie kept going. "No, it's not. It didn't make any sense to get mad. I should have told you what was bothering me."

Nick grinned. "So tell me. Or as Miss T. would say, 'Who put the burr under your saddle?'"

Addie grinned, but she sobered up quickly. "In the last few days, I've discovered there are a lot of people who think Conor *is* a troublemaker. And they don't approve of all the kids the Davises have."

Nick was astonished. "Conor? A troublemaker?" Then he frowned. "What business is it of anyone else how many kids they have?"

Addie nodded in agreement. "That's how I feel. But there are other people who disagree. I think Conor has a hard enough time with them. We're his friends. We don't need to talk about him, too, even if we are joking."

"I'll never say another bad word about him or his family," Nick promised.

"Thanks," Addie said. "Why don't you stay and learn some of the programs with us? I'm sure my mom wouldn't care."

Nick called his mom to tell her he'd be home a little late. He and Addie waited in the front yard for Conor and his mom, but it was Conor and Mr. Mueller who pulled into the McCormicks' drive just a few minutes later.

The computer science teacher greeted Addie and Nick as he stepped from his car. The shock of white hair that traveled back from his forehead never failed to surprise Addie. It was strange to see so much gray hair in a man no older than her father.

"Hi, kids," he said. "Is your mom or dad home, Addie?"

Addie nodded. "My mom is."

Mrs. McCormick had seen the strange car pull in the drive and was already at the front door.

"Mr. Mueller!" she said and shook his hand. "My husband told me of your offer to help with our computer class. That's very kind of you."

"No problem," he said. "Conor told me he was coming out this afternoon, so I offered him a ride. I thought it would be a good time to look over some of the programs you have."

"Please come in," Mrs. McCormick said. She held the front door open and led the little group down the hall to the classroom. She turned the computer on and while they waited for it to boot up, Mrs. McCormick opened the left desk drawer, showing Mr. Mueller the copies of all the different programs Brian had left with them.

"Pretty impressive," he said. "You've got quite a collection here. I have access to several more I'm sure you'd be interested in. I can let you look at them. Then you can make copies of whatever you want."

Mrs. McCormick hesitated. "Isn't that—illegal?"

Mr. Mueller appeared surprised. "Well, technically, yes. But I think the big software companies expect people to 'cheat,'" he said with a wink.

Addie's mother smiled politely, but she shook her head. "I appreciate the opportunity to try the games first, but we'll buy whatever we want to keep."

Mr. Mueller simply shrugged and changed the subject. "It will take some time to show you how to use all these." He looked around for a wall clock, but there was none.

Conor checked the time. "It's almost four," the young man told him.

Nick saw the sparkle of gold on Conor's wrist and he whistled softly. "What a cool watch! Is that a calculator? Where'd you get that?"

Conor seemed embarrassed to answer Nick's questions. "It was a gift to—I mean it's a gift. It's my dad's watch."

Nick was confused. "So which is it? A gift or your dad's?"

Conor laughed uncomfortably. "It was a gift to . . . my father. He lets me wear it sometimes."

Nick knew enough to let the subject drop. Addie stared at the ground, and both the adults regarded the young boy carefully. But Conor refused to meet anyone's eyes. Instead, he pulled the sleeve of his sweatshirt over the watch.

"So which game should we start with?" he asked abruptly.

Mr. Mueller took a deep breath. "Have you done any work with those geography programs yet, Mrs. McCormick?"

Addie's mom shook her head, so the computer science teacher sat down, took the mouse and opened the hard drive, then clicked on the first geography game on the menu.

For the next hour or so, he and Conor worked through the different programs. They showed Mrs. McCormick all the options for a game that took the player, an early pioneer, across the western United

States. It was a fascinating game and soon everyone was absorbed in the dilemmas the pioneer faced as his money ran out, his wife got sick, and coyotes attacked his camp.

Addie's father came home before they were finished. Mr. McCormick greeted Mr. Mueller and offered him a cup of coffee. The three adults went to the kitchen while Conor and Nick continued the game, panning gold in the Rocky Mountains.

Finally Nick sat back. "I've got to quit. My mom's going to have supper ready soon. She'll be mad if I'm late. Can I save my game?"

"I think so," Conor said. But when he went to OPTIONS, there was no save command.

"You mean I did all that work for nothing?" Nick groaned.

"No, I'm sure there's a way to save it," Conor insisted.

"I could ask Mr. Mueller," Addie suggested.

Conor was busy looking through all the different commands under OPTIONS. "Yeah, why don't you do that," he said in an absentminded voice.

Addie slipped out of the room and down the hall to the kitchen. Even before she reached the door, she could hear the subdued voices of her father and Mr. Mueller.

"Please allow Conor to continue using your computer," the teacher was saying. "I know how much it means to him to come here. And since I can't help him anymore this year, I'd like to think your influence on him will keep him in line."

"Of course," Mr. McCormick said. "But if I hear any more rumors about him, I'll have to talk with him—or preferably, his father."

Mr. Mueller sighed deeply. "I can't tell you if those rumors are true or not. I like that boy a lot. But he's certainly been acting strange lately."

CHAPTER 8

A View from the Sky

The last day of the first week of homeschool dawned fresh and clear. At first, Addie was preoccupied with thoughts of Conor and his problems. But the weather was so beautiful and her friends were so full of energy she found it hard to stay depressed for long.

When break time came, they took their snacks out to the yard and sat under the maple tree, laughing and talking. Mrs. McCormick joined them and even she seemed reluctant to go back in when the break was over. Nick came up with a creative alternative.

"Why don't we have our silent reading time now, instead of this afternoon, and sit out here and read?" he asked.

"Yeah!" the other three children chorused.

"And just how well do you think you'd concentrate?" Mrs. McCormick laughed.

"I'll concentrate better," Nick insisted. "If I'm inside, I'll sit and look out the window."

"Me, too," Andy agreed.

"Come on, Mom," Addie begged. "You're not limited to what a teacher with thirty kids has to do. There's only four of us. We'll behave. I promise."

With a shake of her head, Mrs. McCormick yielded to the passionate pleas of the children, and they all ran inside to get their library books. Nick was the fastest, and he claimed a spot on one of the two coveted lawn chairs under the maple tree. Mrs. McCormick took the other, and the remaining three kids spread out in the grass around them.

They read quietly for almost an hour. There were only the sounds of birds chirping, a breeze blowing, an occasional car passing on the country road... and Nick snoring.

Addie did a log roll across the grass and kicked his shoe, hoping to wake him up before her mom heard him. But when they checked Mrs. McCormick, her eyes were closed as well. With as little noise as possible, the four children tiptoed behind the garage and waited for her to wake up.

That's the scene Mr. McCormick found several minutes later when he pulled into the drive just before noon.

"Hey, teach!" he yelled as he slammed the car door.

Mrs. McCormick woke up with a start and looked around her in confusion. "What—where—where did those kids go?"

The children burst out from behind the garage in a gale of laughter.

"Rough morning, Mrs. McCormick?" Mr. McCormick asked with a grin. "Hope we're not working you too hard."

Addie's mom tried to frown at her husband, but a yawn interrupted her and she stood up and stretched. "Well, so much for that experiment," she said. "Silent reading inside from now—"

"Mom, you just fell asleep a few minutes ago. Really!"

"Yeah, Mrs. McCormick, we all read for almost an hour," Hillary chimed in.

Mr. McCormick couldn't resist teasing his wife just a little more. "Oh, you didn't get much of a nap, then. Well, maybe you can lay down after lunch. Call it science. Have the kids do research on the sleep patterns of middle-aged females—"

That was going too far and Mr. McCormick knew it. He took off running, and Mrs. McCormick chased him around the corner of the garage, but not before she grabbed the hose.

Nick checked to make sure the water was turned on. It was, but Addie's father was faster than her mother, and he stood at the edge of the field, just out of reach of the cold spray.

"Truce!" Mr. McCormick shouted. "Truce!"

"Truce nothing," Mrs. McCormick grinned. "What are you doing home, anyway?" she demanded.

"I have a real science project for the kids this afternoon, if you're interested," he said.

Mrs. McCormick was suspicious. "And just what is that?"

"I called our insurance agent this morning to file a claim on the repairs we did to the roof. He told me there have been so many claims since the tornado, the parent company is sending a photographer down here to take aerial pictures of the town. Bill Rankin is going to take him up. So I called the airstrip and talked to Bill. He said he'd be glad to give the kids a ride."

At the mention of a helicopter ride, all the children started to cheer.

"John!" Mrs. McCormick had to shout to be heard over the noise. "We have to check with their parents first—"

"I already called the Jacksons and the Meekers." Mr. McCormick took a few steps toward the garage. "It's fine with them. Nick will have to call his mom."

The older man caught Nick's eye and gave a slight nod of his head toward the water faucet. Nick grinned and slipped quietly around the corner of the garage.

"I've never been in a helicopter myself," Mr. McCormick said, continuing his cautious walk back to the house.

Addie stepped back to see if Nick had turned off the water. But Nick was simply leaning against the garage wall with a smile on his face.

Mrs. McCormick loosened her grip on the nozzle. "This is a wonderful opportunity," she agreed with a smile. "Can I go along?"

"Of course!" Mr. McCormick. "You can go up with Addie and Hillary, and I'll go with the boys."

Then his wife frowned. "There's a lot to do before we leave," she said.

Mr. McCormick looked puzzled. "Like what?"

"You're going to have to change your clothes," she said and turned the hose on him full force.

"Nick!" Mr. McCormick bellowed. "You were supposed to turn that off!"

But Nick was laughing with all the other kids and didn't seem too concerned. Finally he managed to say, "You deserved that, Mr. McCormick!"

"Yeah, I guess I did," the man grinned and shook his wet head like a dog. "But it was worth it!"

* * *

"Everybody been to the bathroom?" the pilot asked bluntly as he handed out yellow molded ear sponges. Addie watched the copilot put his in, and she and the others followed suit.

"If you haven't, go now," he instructed them. "The way the seats vibrate, you don't want to take any chances," he said.

Hillary giggled self-consciously at the instructions. Nick just grinned and headed for the bathroom.

"Let's take the girls first," the pilot shouted over the roar of the helicopter. Addie, Hillary, and Mrs.

McCormick climbed into the huge machine and squeezed into the seat in the back.

Once inside, Addie could feel her whole body vibrating with the Bell Jetranger. With the door closed, much of the noise was shut out, but it was still very loud. Everyone strapped in, and the noise and vibration increased until the helicopter seemed to rock gently from side to side. Then the machine lifted off the ground, tilted forward just a little bit, and skimmed down the runway at Rankin's Airfield. Once they had picked up speed, they climbed high into the air, and the airstrip beneath them looked like a long, gray ribbon.

The motion of the aircraft made Addie's stomach do little loops and twists, but she soon forgot her nervousness. They were flying southwest over acres and acres of fields, freshly plowed and waiting to be planted. She'd always thought all dirt was the same, but in the air she could see variations in color. Different farmers had plowed at different times, and some fields were drier than others. Although there were no fences, there were strips of grass that showed where one farm stopped and another began. From the air it looked as if someone had pieced together a giant quilt.

The copilot motioned above his head. Addie and Hillary looked up to see headsets dangling above them. Mrs. McCormick pulled hers down and adjusted it over her ears. She hit her push-to-talk button and said something to the pilot.

Addie pulled hers down and Hillary did the same. They could hear the tinny voices of the pilot and copilot as they talked about visible flight rules and elevation.

"So what do you think, girls?"

The unexpected question startled Addie, and she looked up to see her mother smiling at them.

Addie hit her push-to-talk button. "Um, this is great," she said hesitantly into the boom mike.

Hillary joined the conversation. "Why are those guys wearing gloves?" she asked.

The pilot heard her and answered the question himself. "These instruments are very sensitive. If my hands get sweaty and slip, we could all be in big trouble! So I wear gloves to absorb the moisture."

The helicopter made a slow turn, and they were flying over Mt. Pilot. Addie gasped in surprise. From the air the damage from the tornado was still very obvious. Although there were signs of repair everywhere they looked, it was much easier to see where roofs had been ripped from buildings and trees had lost their branches.

The school was the worst. The south end didn't look too bad, even though the roof was still missing. But the addition on the north end had collapsed. It didn't even look like a school anymore, just a pile of concrete and rubble.

Addie and Hillary were silent as they watched from the air. They could see the miniature work crews clearly as they scurried around the building with their scoop shovels and dump trucks, clearing away the debris.

Addie looked behind the grade school to the high school. Many of its windows were boarded up and a

large section of the roof was gone, but that building
was in much better shape than the rest of the school.
A solitary car sat in the large parking lot. Suddenly,
a side exit door opened and a man stepped out into
the sunshine.

"Isn't that Mr. Mueller?" Addie asked Hillary.
The man hurrying along the ground was so small
he almost looked unreal, but the black hair and gray
streak that glinted in the sunlight were unmistak-
able.

Hillary nodded. "Wonder what he's doing here?"
she asked. "I thought the school was still off-limits
to the public." She shrugged. "Maybe teachers
aren't considered 'the public.'"

"Yeah, maybe," Addie said. But there were no
other teachers around. Why was Mr. Mueller there?
The tiny figure stepped over the yellow warning
tape and hurried to his car.

Hillary tapped her arm and pointed out the window on the other side. Three deer were grazing at
the edge of a field, hundreds of feet below. As the
chopper flew over them, pounding the air, they
bolted for the wooded area directly behind them.
Addie and Hillary watched until they disappeared
from view.

CHAPTER 9

The Game

It was after three-thirty when Addie, Nick, and her parents left the airport. Mrs. Jackson had been to Rankin's Airfield to watch the flight and take Hillary and Andy home.

Nick talked helicopter jargon nonstop from the moment they left Rankin's. He and Mr. McCormick tossed around words and phrases like "cyclic," "the pitch of the rotor," "the collective button," "compression," "combustion"—all things Addie had heard as well. But she'd been too interested in the view to pay much attention. Now she was embarrassed that Nick had learned so much and she had learned so little.

Her mother saw the look on her face and smiled. "I don't understand it either, hon. I think it's a male thing."

Mr. McCormick heard her comment and wagged his finger at her. "Don't teach our daughter stereotypes," he chided his wife. "How do you know she won't grow up to be a jet fighter pilot?"

Mrs. McCormick ignored him and pointed toward their drive. "I forgot all about Conor!"

Conor Davis was walking around the side of their house. He saw their car and waved. Mr. McCormick honked lightly and pulled up to the garage door.

"Hi, there," Conor said with a grin as Addie and Nick stepped out of the car. "I was beginning to wonder where you were at. When Mom dropped me off, we just assumed you were home. But no one answered the door, so I walked around back to look in the window of the classroom. I thought maybe you didn't hear me knocking."

Mr. McCormick smiled. "Anxious to get to work, are you?"

Conor nodded. "I finally got on the computer at school today, but only for about fifteen minutes." He sighed. "I'll sure be glad when this year is over and we're back at Heritage. I wish we were there now."

"That time will come quicker than you think," Mrs. McCormick laughed. "Meanwhile, you've got me to tutor. Let's go in."

Nick got his bike from the garage and left for home. Addie followed her mother and Conor to the classroom.

They had just turned the computer on when Addie heard the phone ring. Her father answered. Addie kept one ear on the conversation down the hall, while Conor and her mom clicked on *The Oregon Trail* and began a trek across nineteenth-century America.

"Hi, Jim, how are you?" Addie heard her father say. ". . . Fine, thanks . . . Oh, it is? When did that happen? . . . Well, good . . . Oh, I don't want to impose on you, Jim . . . Sure you don't mind? I could bring Addie, maybe Nick, too . . . That's kind of you . . . I appreciate it . . . See you tommorow . . . Thanks . . . Bye."

Addie slipped out of the room and down the hall to talk to her father. "Who was that, Dad?"

"Mr. Mueller," her father replied. "He called to tell us the electricity has been restored at the high school. He thought we might be interested in looking at some of the programs they have. They received some new games a day or two before the tornado hit."

Addie nodded. "That's what he was going to show us in class that afternoon."

"Well, he'll show them to you and Nick tomorrow if you're interested," Mr. McCormick told her.

"But how can he do that?" Addie wanted to know. "I thought the whole system was wiped out in the storm."

Her father nodded. "Most of the software *was* wiped out when the system crashed," he said. "But

they have all their original programs on disk, and
the teachers always made backups of any important
work they did. Mr. Beland, the superintendent,
keeps all that locked in a waterproof, fireproof
vault."

"So they still have all of their programs and
games?" Addie asked.

"Right," Mr. McCormick said. "And most of their
hardware is usable. Only a few units sustained
some water damage. Jim—Mr. Mueller thinks we'll
be able to load the new games back on the system
and take a look at them."

"Great!" Addie ran down the hall to tell Conor
the good news.

Mrs. McCormick was just coming out the door of
the classroom. "I forgot I had clothes in the dryer,
Addie. Why don't you play the game while I fold
them?"

Addie nodded and slipped into the vacant chair
next to Conor. But she didn't pay any attention to
what was happening on the screen. Instead, she
tugged on Conor's shirtsleeve.

"Guess what?" she said excitedly. "Most of the
information that was on the computer system at the
high school is still there!"

"How do you know?" Conor turned away from
his game and gave Addie his full attention.

"Mr. Mueller just called my dad," she said. "He's
going to show us some new games tomorrow. He
told Dad most of the computers are still usable and
all the disks and . . . and backup stuff are locked in a
waterproof, fireproof vault in the superintendent's
office."

Conor did a long drumroll on the desktop and ended with an imaginary *ca-ching* on the cymbals. "I knew it!" he said. "I was sure they had backups somewhere. That means they've probably still got my—" he glanced at Addie, "—my work on disk," he finished lamely.

"Conor!" Addie couldn't control her curiosity any longer. "What's going on? What are you trying to keep secret?"

"What do you mean?" he asked, but he was grinning broadly and his eyes danced.

"The day you and Mr. Mueller came to class I knew there was something special about those games. I could see it in your face. What is it?"

Conor lowered his voice. "Promise you won't tell anyone?"

Addie nodded.

"I wrote one of the games," he said.

Addie's eyes grew wide. "You mean you wrote a computer game all by yourself?" she asked.

Conor nodded proudly. "Mr. Mueller says it's one of the best he's ever seen. I might even be able to sell it."

Addie beamed. "That's wonderful, Conor! But—why don't you want to tell anyone about it?"

"There's a lot of competition in the market, even in a town like Mt. Pilot. Mr. Mueller says there are a lot of hackers out there who would steal it if they knew about it."

Addie made a face. "What's a hacker? It sounds gross."

Conor laughed. "It's just a name for a person who's very good on computers."

"So you're a hacker," Addie concluded.

Conor looked pleased and shocked at the same time. "Well, not really. Hackers usually break into other people's systems and steal their files. I'd never do that. I suppose I could if I wanted to try."

Then he shook his head. "But I wouldn't. And I made my game very hard to steal. You have to know the password to get access to it."

Before Addie could ask the obvious question, Conor grinned. "And no one—*absolutely no one*—knows the password but me."

"Do you think Mr. Mueller might have a copy of your game with the others he brought to class that day?" Addie asked.

Conor shrugged. "I know it was on one of the disks he brought with him, but those disks are gone. He set them on Mrs. Glasgow's desk, remember?"

Addie nodded. She'd seen him do it, and she remembered how he checked his pocket later. "They're history," she agreed. "Would the superintendent have a backup of the game in his vault?"

"I'm almost sure of it." Conor gazed thoughtfully out the classroom window. "I wish I could get to the school myself tomorrow, but I have to work," he said.

"Where are you working?" Addie asked.

Conor hesitated. "It's not a real job," he finally said. "I'm just doing some things for a—friend." He changed the subject quickly. "Addie, would you do me a favor?"

"What?"

"Look for the backup disk that has my game on it."

"But I don't have any idea what I'm looking for!" Addie protested.

"Sure you do," Conor said. "You know what a disk looks like, right? Well, Mr. Mueller marks all his disks the same way. His initials—JAM—are on the top line. The class name and the date are on the second line. Then there's a brief description of the contents on the last line."

Addie frowned. "I don't know, Conor. I can't just waltz in and open the vault."

Conor kept talking as if he hadn't heard her. "I finished the game the day before spring break, so look for a disk that says JAM, Computer Science, March 15, and then my name, or my initials and the word game, something like that. Got it?"

Addie sighed. "I suppose I could ask Mr. Beland if—"

"Don't ask!" Conor interrupted her hastily.

"Why not?"

"Mr. Mueller thinks some of the hackers might be right in our own school," he said reluctantly.

"Why can't you ask Mr. Mueller to find the game for you?" she wanted to know.

"I already did," Conor said. "He told me we had to wait until he had free access to all the computer files. He didn't want to arouse anyone's suspicions."

Addie shook her head. "There's something about this that just doesn't feel right, Conor," she said.

"Please, Addie," the older boy begged. "I'm not asking you to take it. Just *look* for it. I just want to know if it's still there. Please."

Addie sighed and nodded. "Okay, I'll look. I'll *try* to look. That's all I'll promise."

The next morning Mr. Mueller met Addie, Nick, and her father at the entrance to the high school. He and Mr. McCormick talked quietly as he led the small group down the hall to the superintendent's office. The school was deserted and the halls were dark. Addie realized it was because plywood had been nailed over all the broken windows, and no light came in through the classrooms.

The four of them met Mr. Beland in his office. Mr. Beland was an older man and a member of Addie's church, although Addie didn't think he attended very often. He rose from his desk and shook hands with Mr. McCormick. Then he pulled a huge set of keys from his belt and opened a small paneled door behind him. When he opened it, Addie saw trays and trays of blue floppy disks.

Mr. Mueller pulled out one tray that had a large white label on the side with the words COMPUTER SCIENCE printed in big black letters. He found the disks he wanted in short order and returned the tray to the vault. The door swung shut but it didn't catch.

I don't care if it shuts or not, she told herself. *There's no way I can look through those disks.*

"We'll take these to my room and work on them," Mr. Mueller told the superintendent. "I've got the instruction manuals on my desk."

"Mind if I tag along?" Mr. Beland asked. "I'd like to talk to Mr. McCormick about homeschooling while he's here."

The five of them walked down the long hall and turned a corner. Mr. Mueller's room was on the left. The only evidence of tornado damage was the plywood over every window. Otherwise, things were in good order.

Mr. Mueller sat down and turned on his computer. While he inserted the disk and copied the programs, Mr. Beland and Addie's father began talking about the McCormicks' unusual school situation.

"Dad," Addie interrupted her father before the conversation could get a real start. "I have to use the bathroom. I'll be right back."

He nodded, and Addie hurried out the door and back down the hall toward the office. Her footsteps sounded incredibly loud in the empty hallway.

Why am I doing this? I could get in big trouble! How will I explain myself if I get caught? But she didn't stop until she reached Mr. Beland's door. She opened it quickly and stepped inside.

I can't do this! I just can't . . . But I'm not really doing anything wrong. I'm just looking around. And I promised Conor.

Just then the swivel chair behind Mr. Beland's desk began to turn slowly. Addie stifled a gasp and backed into the door so fast she hit her head.

The chair stopped suddenly. Addie took a deep breath, then stepped forward and peered cautiously over the top of the desk.

Conor Davis was crouching behind the chair. His frightened blue eyes peered up at her out of a very pale face.

CHAPTER 10

Who's Telling
the Truth?

Addie was so relieved she felt her knees buckle underneath her, and she leaned on the desk for support.

"What are you doing here?" she managed to squeak out.

Conor sat down—hard—on the floor and took a deep breath before he answered. "I felt bad last night. I knew it was wrong to ask you to sneak around like this. So I decided to come by the school before work and ask Mr. Mueller if he'd found my game."

Addie was suspicious. "Then why are you in here?"

"I was going to ask him, really I was!" Conor insisted. "But when I saw all of you go around the corner into the computer science room, it was just too much of a temptation. I had to look for myself."

He held up a disk and grinned triumphantly. "Here it is, Addie! I found it."

Addie smiled at his excitement. "Well, I'm glad. Put it back, and we'll go tell Mr. Mueller it's here."

Conor shook his head vehemently. "I'll get in big trouble if they know I got into the vault without permission. So will you," he added.

Addie's heart began to pound again. He was right. If her father found out she'd lied about the bathroom to sneak into the superintendent's office, there would be a price to pay.

How do I get myself into these things? she thought. *I'm sorry, Lord. I'll never do this again. Just help us get out of here without getting caught.*

Addie opened the door to the hall cautiously. Still deserted. She motioned to Conor. "Put that disk back and let's go. If they think you just got here, we won't get in trouble. Then you can come back to the office with Mr. Mueller when we leave and get your game."

Conor nodded. He put the disk back in the tray and closed the door to the vault. This time it clicked shut. Together they slipped quietly into the hall and walked back around the corner to the computer science room.

Mr. Beland smiled warmly when Conor walked into the room with Addie. "Good to see you, Conor!

But I'm not surprised. John's told me how much you're helping Mrs. McCormick with her new 'school.' I'm glad they invited you along."

Since Conor hadn't been invited, there was an awkward silence, but Mr. Beland didn't notice it. Mr. Mueller covered the situation smoothly.

"Good morning, Conor," he said with a glance at his watch. "You're a busy guy this morning. Aren't you supposed to be at Blacker's at ten o'clock?"

Conor nodded. "I—I just wanted to see what games we—we might be using next week," he stammered.

Addie's father spoke up. "You haven't got much time," he said. "Do you need a ride?"

"No," Conor said. "I've got my bike. I guess I'll be going." He glanced at Addie and Nick. "I'll see you tomorrow. Mom says we're going to visit your church."

"See you then," Nick said.

Mr. Beland walked with Conor out the door, and Addie breathed a sigh of relief. At least he wouldn't be tempted to go back to the office with Mr. Beland escorting him.

Addie took a seat next to Nick and listened carefully for the next hour as Mr. Mueller opened up the new math games and the history game and showed the two children all the different options available. Then he copied the games onto a blank disk and handed it to Mr. McCormick.

"Take your time learning them," he said.

"We'll return this disk when we've decided which ones we might use," Mr. McCormick said. "Do you have a catalog I can order from?" he asked.

Mr. Mueller nodded. "Sure. I have several." He hesitated and Addie wondered if he was going to offer to let them "cheat" again. But all he said was, "Just let me know which games you want."

They walked back to the office. Mr. Beland stood to tell the McCormicks and Nick goodbye. Mr. Mueller walked behind the desk to return the floppy disks to the vault. He tried the handle, but the door was shut and locked once more.

"I thought I left that open," Mr. Beland mused. "Got your key, Jim?"

Mr. Mueller nodded and pulled a handful of keys from his pocket. He opened the vault and returned the disks to the COMPUTER SCIENCE tray. He flipped casually through several more disks, and Addie watched him closely.

"Were those the only games you had to show us in class that day?" she asked quickly, before she lost her nerve.

Mr. Mueller turned and gave her a studied look. "That was it," he said. "Why do you ask?"

"You told us you had a surprise," Nick said. "Conor said it was something you worked on in one of your computer programming classes."

"Oh, that," Mr. Mueller nodded. "I helped some students write a game we wanted you to try. It was still pretty rough, but I thought you might enjoy it. I'm afraid I left the only copy I had on Mrs. Glasgow's desk that afternoon. And you know what happened to that," he said with a grim smile.

Nick nodded. "It's—gone with the wind," he said in a dramatic voice.

Everyone groaned at Nick's bad joke, but Addie paid little attention. Her thoughts were racing.

Mr. Mueller helped write it? With several other students? Conor said he wrote it all by himself! And Mr. Mueller said it was rough, but Conor claimed it was "one of the best" Mr. Mueller had ever seen. And Mr. Mueller said there wasn't a copy—so what was Conor looking for? What was really on the disk he showed me?

Addie's spirits drooped as her mind kept coming back to the only logical conclusion. Conor was lying. But why? What was he trying to hide?

She followed her dad and the others out the door and into the parking lot. She was so lost in thought Nick had to poke her twice to get her attention. "What's with you all of a sudden?" he asked.

Addie shook her head. "I don't want to talk about it right now. I haven't figured it out myself. I'll tell you later."

Nick could hear the dejection in her voice, and he didn't ask any more questions. He turned his attention back to Addie's father and Mr. Mueller.

"When did Conor start working at Blacker's?" Mr. McCormick asked the teacher.

"He doesn't have a job there," Mr. Mueller said slowly. "He owes Mr. Blacker some money, so he's working it off every Saturday."

Mr. McCormick made no comment, but Addie could see the look of concern on his face and her heart sank even further. Conor *had* been involved in the looting at Blacker's Jewelry Store! Why else would he owe Mr. Blacker money?

And the worst part is, I have to face Conor at church tomorrow! How can I even look him in the eye?

Her thoughts made her so sad, she blinked back tears and didn't say a word all the way home.

* * *

The next morning, Addie, along with the rest of the church, watched all nine members of the Davis family file into one of the pews at the front of the church. The men wore suits (even Sean had a bow tie on), and the four little girls wore ruffly dresses. Mrs. Davis looked trim and pretty in a simple blue dress. Addie studied the woman's figure carefully but could see no signs of pregnancy. Mrs. McCormick saw her staring, and she nudged her daughter with a slight frown.

Addie blushed and shrugged. She wasn't the only one staring. Mrs. Kreiling was practically hanging over two pews trying to get a better look at the family.

Mr. Sadler, one of the elders, walked up to the podium and opened the service with prayer and a passage from the book of Proverbs. As happened so often, the passage he chose was aimed directly at Addie's heart.

"He whose walk is upright fears the Lord, but he whose ways are devious despises him. A truthful witness does not deceive, but a false witness pours out lies."

That sounds like Conor, was Addie's first thought and then the truth hit her. *Conor? CONOR? What about you? You lied to everyone yesterday so you could sneak into the office and look through Mr. Beland's vault.*

Then you prayed and asked the Lord to help you get away with it!

A small part of Addie wanted to argue, to make excuses. She had only done it to help her friend. But the Spirit of the Lord was persistent.

If you really want to help him, you need to be honest. Covering his lies won't help him at all.

Addie closed her eyes. *I'm sorry, Lord. Please forgive me. I'll tell Dad the truth as soon as I can.*

Addie's opportunity to "'fess up" came sooner than she expected. During the break that morning she saw her father and Mr. Beland talking at the back of the church. She made her way to her father's side and got in on the tail end of a disturbing conversation.

"It seemed like too much of a coincidence. No one, not even me, has been in that office for more than two weeks. And I know those disks weren't missing when I opened the vault the first time."

Mr. McCormick nodded. "I'll talk to the boy."

Both men looked to the front of the church. Conor and his family were still in their pew, talking to several other members of the church who had stopped by to greet them.

"I don't think now is the right time," Mr. McCormick said, "but we see quite a bit of Conor and his mother on school days. I'll find out what I can."

"Thanks." Mr. Beland smiled at Addie and patted her shoulder, then he rejoined his wife.

Mr. McCormick looked carefully at his young daughter. "Did you hear what that was about?" he asked her quietly.

Addie nodded.

"Is there anything you can tell me?"

Addie took a deep breath. "There's a lot I have to tell you, Dad."

CHAPTER 11

Troubling Evidence

"We'll talk at lunch," was Mr. McCormick's only comment before the worship time began. Usually Addie loved singing songs of praise, but today she had a difficult time keeping her mind on the music. When the service was finally over, she tried to get out the back door before Conor could see her, but she didn't make it. Hillary stopped her, and Conor caught up with both of them at the rear of the church. Nick joined them.

"Hi, Conor," Hillary said.

"Hi," he said shortly. "Say, Addie, did you and Nick get to try those games yesterday?"

Addie nodded, but she avoided looking at the older boy. "Yeah, they were fun. Nothing special, though."

Conor understood her meaning, and he sighed.

"What games?" Hillary asked.

"We went to the high school yesterday with Addie's father," Nick said. "Mr. Mueller showed us the games he was going to teach our class that last day of school."

"Really?" Hillary said. "I heard Mrs. Beland tell my mom they think someone broke into the high school over the weekend. There are some things missing from Mr. Beland's office."

Addie nodded. "Some computer disks," she said. "Mr. Beland told my dad about it this morning." She risked a glance at Conor. His eyes were wide and his face was pale.

"Addie—" he sputtered.

But Addie wouldn't look at him. He flushed a deep red from the neck up, and his expression grew fierce. He turned and pushed his way through the people who still lingered by the back door. The three children watched him leave.

"What was that all about?" Hillary asked.

Nick scowled at Addie. "Would you tell us what's going on?" he demanded. "Something's up and you know what it is!"

Addie hesitated. "I'll tell you tomorrow at school— if I can." She hurried out the back door herself, anxious to avoid any more questions.

*　*　*

Addie and her parents went to a local deli for lunch, and Addie ordered her favorite submarine sandwich—seafood and crabmeat on whole wheat bread. But she only nibbled at her food, and Mrs. McCormick was concerned.

"Are you feeling okay, hon?" she asked her daughter.

Mr. McCormick spoke before Addie could answer. "I think she has a bad case of the 'guilts,'" he said. "Do you know what happened to the disks in Mr. Beland's office, Addie?"

"No," she answered honestly. "Not for sure. But I have a guess."

She told her parents the entire story, starting with the day of the tornado and her hunch that there was something special about the games Mr. Mueller brought to class that day. She reminded them of the night the Davises came to supper and repeated Conor's comments about his work with Mr. Mueller in computer programming. Finally she came to her conversation with Conor on Friday afternoon.

"He told me it wasn't just another game—it was a game *he* wrote," she said. "But he was afraid it had been destroyed when the system crashed during the tornado. When I told him most of the information on the computers had been saved, he was thrilled." Addie hesitated.

"And . . ." her father prodded.

"And he asked me to look for the backup disk that his game was on," Addie said.

Both her parents were staring at her, and Addie hurried to reassure them. "Oh, I didn't take it. I didn't even look for it," she said. Then she admitted, "I was going to look for it when I told you I was going to the bathroom yesterday at the high school. But Conor was already in Mr. Beland's office. And he said he found the disk that had his game on it."

Mr. and Mrs. McCormick were silent for quite a long time. Finally her mother spoke. "Addie, you could have gotten in a lot of trouble yesterday. I know you wouldn't steal anything—I know you didn't steal anything," she corrected herself. "But going into the office of a school official and looking through school property in a locked vault is *very wrong.*"

"It's criminal," her father said roughly. "If they caught an adult doing that, they'd be arrested. And it doesn't matter how pure your motives or how good your intentions are," he added. "It's wrong."

Addie nodded, close to tears. "I know. I'm sorry."

"You're grounded for the next week," her father said in a quieter voice. "No friends over after school."

Addie swallowed hard but didn't argue.

"What I don't understand is why this game is so important to Conor that he has to steal it from the school," Mr. McCormick continued. "Why can't he just wait and get it from Mr. Mueller? I'm sure Jim would be glad to give him a copy."

Addie sighed. "That's the other part of the story, Dad. I'm not sure Conor is telling the truth. He told me this was a game he had written all by himself. He said it was one of the best Mr. Mueller had ever seen. But when we asked Mr. Mueller about it Saturday, he said he helped *several* students write the program. He even said it wasn't very good, but he thought we'd enjoy it."

Mr. McCormick nodded. "I remember that. He also said the copy he took to your class the day of the tornado was the only copy he had."

"Right," Addie said. "So what was on the disk Conor showed me yesterday morning? What did he really steal from the office?"

"This does not sound like the Conor Davis I know," Mrs. McCormick said incredulously. "I can't understand why he'd do such a thing!"

"Money," Mr. McCormick said simply. "You can sell computer games and programs well below market prices and still make a lot of money. It's called pirating. Usually people use their computers to steal electronically from another person's files."

"Hackers," Addie said softly.

"You've heard of 'em, huh?" her father asked.

"From Conor." Addie began wrapping her sub up in a napkin. "We'd better get a doggie bag for this," she said. "I'm not very hungry."

* * *

The next morning Nick, Andy, and Hillary cornered Addie in the backyard during break.

"Okay, out with it," Nick demanded. He gave her arm a gentle twist. "Or I'll have one a da boys work ya over," he said in his best gangster voice.

Addie didn't laugh, and Nick dropped her arm with a frown. "What's going on, for Pete's sake?"

Addie related the same chain of events she had described to her parents the previous day. The other children listened in silence. When she was finished, no one knew what to say.

Finally Nick spoke. "I agree with your mom. That's not the Conor Davis we know."

Addie shrugged. "I don't know what to think of him anymore. I didn't believe he looted Blacker's Jewelry Store either, but evidently he did. He's working for Mr. Blacker on Saturdays to pay off the money he owes him."

"That doesn't make sense," Andy said. "If he really stole that watch from Blacker's, why does he still have it? Wouldn't you think they'd make him give it back?"

Addie stared at her friend. "Yeah," she said slowly. "You're right."

"He said it was a gift to his father," Nick put in. "I believe him. And he left that watch by the computer. It's got a timer on it. We were playing one of the spelling games Thursday, and Conor took it off so we could time ourselves. It's still sitting there."

"Let's take a look at it," Addie said.

The four children ran back into the classroom. The watch was sitting just where Nick had said. He picked it up and examined it. Then he gave an excited shout and stuck his tongue out at Addie.

"Told you so," he said with a satisfied smile. "*To Dad, From C, L, A, M, B, K, & S,*'" he read off the back and did a doubletake. "Wonder if they know their initials spell 'clambakes?'" he muttered.

Hillary giggled. "Who cares, Nick?" she said. "The important thing is that it proves it was a gift from the kids to their dad. Conor must be working for Mr. Blacker to pay off what they owe on the watch."

"Right," Nick said. "So if you're wrong about the watch, Addie, maybe you're wrong about the games, too."

Addie took the watch and studied the back. *C, L, A, M, B, K, & S.* Conor, Liam, Annie, Mary, Bridget, Kerry, and Sean. There was no mistaking the inscription. She rubbed one finger over the engraving and prayed silently.

Oh, Lord, I'd love to be wrong about everything! I don't want to believe the worst about Conor. I want to believe he's as nice as I always thought he was. But it doesn't look good. And I think You're the only One who can make it look better.

CHAPTER 12

A Chance Meeting

After art class at the Bradys', Addie rode her bike home alone. It was going to be a long week, spending afternoons by herself. She went inside and ate two chocolate chip cookies with a glass of orange juice at the kitchen table.

Mrs. McCormick came up the basement stairs with a basket full of towels. "Hi, honey," she said cheerfully. "How was art?" Without waiting for an answer, she asked her daughter, "Would you like to go in town to the mall with me? I've got to buy a spring coat and Marketplace is having a sidewalk sale today."

"Sure, I'll go," Addie said. Normally, shopping was not her favorite thing to do, but it beat staying home by herself without any friends.

Marketplace Shopping Center, at the northeast edge of town, was one of the few areas in Mt. Pilot that had not been damaged by the tornado. The parking lot was crowded, and Mrs. McCormick parked far from the entrance.

"Where's the sale?" Addie asked.

"What?"

"The sidewalk sale. I don't see anything out here."

Her mother laughed. "I'm afraid that's just a figure of speech anymore," she said. "Now that stores are all inside, they have their sales inside as well."

The "sidewalks" in the mall were jammed with people examining the racks of clothes and other merchandise storeowners had set out for the sale. Addie tired quickly of fighting the crowd and tapped her mother on the shoulder.

"Do you mind if I sit on that bench and read?" she asked.

Mrs. McCormick laughed. "Not at all, honey." She glanced at her watch. "I'll meet you there in half-an-hour. Forty-five minutes at the most."

Addie just grinned as she made her way to the relative quiet of the sunken rest area in the center of the mall. That meant she had at least an hour to read, maybe more. Her mother had a "shop-till-you-drop" mentality, and Addie had finished lots of good books in a variety of malls.

She settled comfortably on the padded bench and pulled her paperback from her jacket pocket. But the noise and activity all around her were too distracting, and she found herself studying different people as they walked by. Then a serious-looking man with a familiar streak of gray hair entered the computer software business across from the rest area, and Addie jammed her book back in her pocket.

She jumped up and followed Mr. Mueller into the store. He was already deep in conversation with a man in a suit and tie. Addie browsed through the store, reading the descriptions of various games, waiting for the teacher to finish his discussion.

What am I going to say to him? she wondered. Deep down, she knew she was hoping he could help her figure out what was going on with Conor.

The two men finished their conversation. Mr. Mueller turned to find Addie staring at him, and he nodded slightly.

Addie smiled. "Hi, Mr. Mueller," she said. She pointed to a boy playing *Tetris* on one of the computers set up in the store. "Conor taught us *Tetris*," she told the computer science teacher, just to make conversation.

Mr. Mueller smiled. "Conor's very good at the game."

Addie nodded. "So is Nick." She watched the different shapes fall faster and faster as the boy advanced another level. She took her eyes off the screen and shook her head. "It's addictive."

"Yes, it is," Mr. Mueller agreed. "Who's got the highest score so far, Nick or Conor?"

Addie shrugged. "I'm not sure. They keep track of their scores, but they never use their real names.

Nick always calls himself *He-man* or *Mastermind*, crazy things like that."

Mr. Mueller laughed. "What does Conor call himself?" he asked casually.

Addie frowned. "I don't remember. His names aren't very . . . flashy."

Mr. Mueller nodded. "That sounds like Conor. He's a pretty quiet kid. I'm never sure what he's thinking." He hesitated. "How are things going? Is he helping you quite a bit?"

"Oh, he helps us a lot," Addie assured the teacher. She hesitated as well, unsure of what to ask or how to ask it.

"Good." Mr. Mueller spoke briskly. "I'm glad to hear it. Goodbye, Addie."

"Bye," said Addie softly, but Mr. Mueller had already turned and was out the door to the mall before she finished speaking.

That really helped, she thought glumly. She left the store and went back to the bench in the rest area to wait for her mother.

An hour later Mrs. McCormick dropped onto the bench next to Addie. She plopped several sacks on the floor between her feet.

Addie peered into each one. The first held a new pair of tennis shoes and several pairs of tube socks for her father. Another held several smaller bags of fragrant coffee beans, and the third was filled with long-sleeved turtlenecks of all different colors.

"Mom . . ." Addie began.

"Sears had a sale," Mrs. McCormick said before Addie could finish.

"*Everyone's* having a sale, Mom," her daughter reminded her. "Where's your coat?"

Mrs. McCormick sighed. "I couldn't decide. Would you come back and look at them with me?"

Addie grinned. "Sure. If I tell you which one to buy, can we go home?"

Her mother laughed. "If you can tell me which one to buy, I'll pick up fried chicken for supper."

Fried chicken was one of Addie's favorite meals, so she waited patiently while her mother tried on a number of coats in two different stores. They eventually decided on a long, navy-blue, all-weather coat with padded shoulders and a rose and blue scarf.

Mrs. McCormick wore her new coat home, and Addie carried the fried chicken inside so her mother wouldn't get greasy. She reached for the doorknob, but the door swung open at her touch, and Addie stepped inside. Her mother followed with all the shopping bags.

"The door was open," Addie said.

Mrs. McCormick nodded. "I left it unlocked. Your dad forgot his keys this morning, and I thought he might beat us home." She frowned. "But I'm sure I pulled it shut when we left."

Addie stuck the chicken in the oven and turned it to "warm." She headed down the hall to the stairs, past the classroom. Then she stopped and walked back to the classroom door. She flicked the light on and peered cautiously into the room.

Something was wrong. She couldn't put her finger on it, but something was wrong. She crossed the room slowly. The chair to the computer was pulled out from the desk, and the metal file that held the worksheets for the different computer programs was not in its usual place. Addie pushed the chair in and slid the file to the back of the desk near the computer. Then she left the room, turning out the light as she went.

She climbed the stairs to her room, feeling troubled and uneasy. She hung her coat up and suddenly realized the reason for her discomfort. She ran from her room and thundered down the stairs, back to the classroom.

She threw the light switch and ran across the room to the desk. Reaching past the metal file to the computer, she ran her hand over the side and across the top of the machine. It was warm!

"Mom!" she shouted.

She must have sounded as scared as she felt, because her mother appeared in the doorway almost immediately.

"Addie," her mother said breathlessly, "what in the world is the matter?"

"Someone's been in our house," Addie informed her mother solemnly.

"What?"

"The front door was open," Addie began.

"I left it unlocked," her mother reminded her.

"But not *open*," Addie said. "And the chair to the computer was pulled out, the file was moved—"

"Addie," her mother interrupted her, "we probably left it like that."

Addie shook her head. "But we didn't leave the

computer on. We've been gone more than two hours. The computer's turned off now, but it's still warm. It shouldn't be warm after *two hours!* Someone's been here."

CHAPTER 13

"Somebody's Been Playing Games"

Mrs. McCormick crossed the room and ran her hand over the top of the computer. A troubled look crossed her face, and she took a deep breath. "Maybe your father has been home," she said.

"Where is he now?" Addie wanted to know. "Why did he leave? And why would he be on the computer?"

"You know he likes to play those games as well as you do," her mother said.

"So Dad came home in the middle of the afternoon to play on the computer and then left before we could catch him?" Addie rolled her eyes. "I don't think so."

Mrs. McCormick frowned at her daughter. "Don't be sarcastic, Addie. I'm just trying to think of the most reasonable explanation for this."

"Sorry," Addie apologized.

"Do you think Conor was here?" Mrs. McCormick mused. "Maybe he came out after school. No one was home, but the door was open, so he came in to use the computer anyway." Then she shook her head. "No, I'm sure I told him I was going shopping this afternoon. I said we could start up again on Tuesday." She paused. "Unless he came out specifically because he *knew* we'd be gone."

"Mom!" Addie was shocked. It wasn't like her mother to accuse someone of wrongdoing before she had the facts.

Mrs. McCormick was embarrassed. "Oh, honey, I'm sorry I said that." She sighed. "I just hate feeling this suspicious about a boy like Conor. He really is such a nice kid."

She glanced nervously around the room. "I suppose we should check the rest of the house, just to make sure our 'visitor' is gone."

Addie's eyes widened. It hadn't occurred to her that the intruder might still be in the house. Her stomach did a quick flip-flop and she swallowed hard. "Where should we check first?" she asked.

Mrs. McCormick straightened her shoulders and in a firm voice said, "Let's start in the basement." Then she closed her eyes briefly and murmured, *"Lord, protect us."*

Addie offered a heartfelt *"Amen,"* and together they got the flashlight from the shelf in the kitchen and opened the basement door.

Mrs. McCormick went first and walked softly down the steps. She was almost at the bottom when she stopped and said in a disgusted tone, "Gwen, use your head and stop being so melodramatic about this. Addie, why don't you go back up and turn the light on?"

Addie giggled and ran swiftly up the stairs. She flicked the switch and the basement was suddenly lit by the soft light of three overhead bulbs. Their basement was one big room with a cement floor and brick walls. It was very cool, and Addie shivered as she came back down the stairs.

Mrs. McCormick marched down the rest of the steps and turned her flashlight on. "There's only one hiding place down here," she said in a loud voice and shined the light behind the furnace. It was empty, except for a cobweb and a Nerf arrow from Nick's bow and arrow set.

Addie breathed a sigh of relief and picked the arrow up. She wiped it off on her jeans and stuck it in her back pocket. "Let's go—" she began to say, but a noise upstairs made her catch her breath.

Mrs. McCormick heard it too, and she put a finger to her lips. Soft footsteps crossed the kitchen floor and stopped at the basement door.

Then the lights in the basement went out and the door slammed shut. Addie stifled a terrified squeal and groped desperately for her mother's hand. She found it in the blackness, and Mrs. McCormick reached out and pulled Addie close.

Then the basement door opened once more. "Hello, Lucy, I'm home," called Mr. McCormick in his best Ricky Ricardo voice. Addie sagged with relief as the lights came back on.

Mr. McCormick trotted down the basement stairs, grinning. "Did I scare—" He stopped when he saw the obvious relief on his wife's and daughter's faces. "I *did* scare you! What's the matter?"

Mrs. McCormick explained the situation as briefly as possible. When she was finished, she paused and said, "Don't ever do that again!"

"I won't," Mr. McCormick promised. "If you promise never to check the house for intruders when I'm gone. It's too dangerous. Stay here while I take a look around."

He was back in less than five minutes. "All clear," he called from the top of the stairs. Addie and her mother joined him, and together they went back to the classroom. Mr. McCormick ran his hand over the computer. Although it had cooled considerably, there was still a warm spot on the side and the top.

Mr. McCormick sat down and flipped the toggle switch on the back of the machine.

"What are you doing?" his wife asked.

"There's an easy way to check and see if someone has been here," he said.

Addie snapped her fingers. "That's right! Every time someone opens a file, the computer records the date and time on the hard drive."

They all waited in silence as the computer booted up. When the hard drive icon came on the screen, Mr. McCormick double-clicked on it, and the menu appeared to the left.

"There it is," Mr. McCormick said softly. He pointed to the dates and times next to a variety of files. "Somebody's been playing games. *The Oregon Trail*, *Freedom*, *Tetris*, *SimCity*..." He paused and looked at his watch. "According to this, they were here about twenty-five minutes ago."

Addie frowned. "But they didn't have time to play the games, Dad." She pointed once more at the times recorded next to the files. "Look at this. *Oregon Trail* was opened at 4:36. *Freedom* was opened at 4:40. *Tetris* at 4:45 and *SimCity* at 4:47. I've played all those games before. It takes much longer than five or ten minutes to play even one of them."

Mr. McCormick nodded slowly. "You're right," he said. "So they weren't playing the games." He paused. "Why would anyone want to open these games and not play them?"

Addie just shook her head.

Mr. McCormick closed the hard drive and hit the SHUT DOWN command. The computer shut off with a soft sigh. Mr. McCormick matched it with a sigh of his own. "This has gone too far. I'm going to have to call Conor's parents tonight."

"Dad," Addie protested, "I don't think it was Conor!"

"Who else would it be?" her father asked.

Addie hesitated. Instead of answering his question, she simply said, "Please don't call Conor's parents until after supper. Give me a chance to think about this until then, okay? Please?"

Mr. McCormick looked from his wife to his daughter and back to his wife. Mrs. McCormick shrugged. "Okay," he relented. "After supper."

"Thanks, Dad," Addie said. She grabbed her blue notebook from the shelf and headed out the door. "Call me when we're ready to eat, Mom."

Addie slipped upstairs to her room. For the next twenty minutes, she scribbled notes and reorganized them, leaving a pile of crumpled-up papers in a heap around her garbage can. When her mother called her for supper, she was just finishing a final copy of her project.

She ran downstairs to the kitchen and tossed her notebook on the counter. She set out the plates and silverware while her mother dished up the food. Her father joined them at the table, and they blessed the meal. The "Amen" was barely out of Addie's mouth before she started talking.

"I've been doing a lot of thinking," she began.

"We're in trouble now," her father muttered under his breath.

Addie ignored him. "Just listen," she said. "Give me a chance, and I think I can prove we've been completely wrong about Conor."

CHAPTER 14

Examining the Evidence

Her parents exchanged a wary glance. "Well, kiddo," her father said slowly, "it certainly doesn't appear that way. He's got a lot of evidence against him."

"Not really, Dad," Addie said. "Not if you take everything we know and really think it through," she insisted.

She turned to her mother. "Remember the day Mrs. Kreiling told us all those awful things about Conor? You said afterwards we shouldn't let gossip influence the way we think about him. But we have, and I can prove it!"

She pulled Conor's watch out of her jeans pocket. "He left this here Thursday. After we listened to Mrs. Kreiling, we saw Conor's new watch and just assumed he stole it. On Saturday, Mr. Mueller told us Conor had to work for Mr. Blacker to pay off the money he owed him."

She turned back to her father. "I don't know about you, but I took that to mean he was involved in the looting and he got caught. Well, I was wrong. Look!"

Mr. McCormick took the watch and examined the inscription. "'To Dad, From C, L, A, M, B, K, & S,'" he read. "That spells 'clambakes,'" he said in a puzzled voice.

Addie grinned. "That's what Nick said."

"Great," her father muttered. "Now I'm starting to think like Nick."

"Those are the initials of all the Davises' kids," Addie said. "Conor is working for Mr. Blacker to pay off what they owe on the watch."

Mrs. McCormick nodded. "I'll bet you're right, Addie."

"So if we were wrong about the watch, we could be wrong about the other things," Addie suggested. She reached for her notebook. "I've written down all the evidence we have for and against Conor."

She turned the notebook around so her parents could see it. "There are only two things we know for certain that go against Conor." She flipped the notebook back around and read from her list.

"'Number one: Mrs. Kreiling doesn't trust him.' That's just her opinion. She's entitled to her opinion, but that doesn't mean she's right.'"

Mr. and Mrs. McCormick exchanged an amused glance, but Addie was too busy reading to notice.

"'Number two: I found Conor hiding in Mr. Beland's office, looking through the computer disks.'" She sighed. "That's a fact. We know that for sure." Then she brightened. "But listen to all the things we have *for* Conor.

"'Number one: We were wrong about the watch.' That's important. The only reason we were suspicious of Conor in the first place is because we thought he stole the watch.

"'Number two: Conor *asked* me to look for his game.' That doesn't make any sense if there wasn't a game to find. I mean, why would he ask me to look for something that wasn't there?"

Addie looked to her parents for an answer, but Mrs. McCormick was silent. "Keep going," was all her father said.

Addie took a deep breath. "'Number three: When I found Conor in the office, he had a disk in his hand and he was very excited because he'd found it.'" She paused. "I suppose that can't be considered real evidence. It just never occurred to me he might be lying. He seemed genuinely happy. I don't think he was there to steal anything. He really did find his game. But that's just *my* opinion."

She continued. "'Number four: I saw Conor put that disk back in the tray in the vault. When he left the building, Mr. Beland was with him, so he couldn't have taken anything then.' When did he have another opportunity to steal those programs?"

She closed her notebook. "That's it," she said.

Mr. McCormick reached out and took his daughter's hand. "Honey, everything you said makes sense, up to a point. But you've left out some hard facts that we have to face. There *are* disks missing from Mr. Beland's office, someone did log onto our computer, and Conor is the only suspect we have."

Addie didn't answer. She picked up her fork and pulled a piece of crispy skin off her chicken.

Mr. McCormick studied his daughter carefully. "Conor *is* our only suspect, right?" He picked up Addie's notebook. She made a grab for it, but he turned the page before she could stop him.

Mr. McCormick's eyes widened in disbelief. "Oh, Addie. You're not serious! Mr. Mueller?!"

"What?" Mrs. McCormick snatched the notebook from her husband. "Addie!"

Addie swallowed hard. "Just listen, okay? Don't say anything. Just listen."

Her parents were still staring at her so Addie hurried into her explanation. "Conor never wanted to keep his game a secret. Mr. Mueller told him they had to keep it quiet because of hackers who might steal it.

"We also know Mr. Mueller is 'moonlighting' for a software company in Chicago. He does research and development, right? He'd always be looking for new games. And—" Addie paused, unwilling to go on.

"Well . . ." her father prodded her.

"We know Mr. Mueller's not completely trust-worthy," Addie continued softly.

"How do we know that?" Mr. McCormick demanded.

"He offered to *give* Mom a copy of those games from the school. He admitted it was illegal, but he said everybody did it."

Mr. McCormick looked at his wife and she nodded slowly. "That bothered me, too," she admitted.

"And Mr. Beland told you yesterday no one else had been in his office since the tornado. But when we flew over the school in the helicopter, Hillary and I saw Mr. Mueller coming out of the school."

Mrs. McCormick verified her daughter's words. "I saw him, too. That gray streak is hard to miss, even from the air."

"There's one more thing," Addie said. "I saw Mr. Mueller at the mall this afternoon when we first arrived. He was at the software store. We talked a little bit about Conor. I told him Conor and Nick were always trying to beat one another in *Tetris*. *Tetris* was one of the games that had been opened, remember?"

Mr. McCormick frowned. "Addie, why would Jim Mueller come out here, enter our house uninvited, and open up *Tetris*?"

Addie took a deep breath. "First off, he knew we weren't home, so there'd be no one here to ask him any questions. Second, Conor told me his game can't be opened without a password. This afternoon, Mr. Mueller asked me what name Conor uses on his scoresheets for the different games. I couldn't remember, and I didn't think much about it at the time. But now I can't help but wonder if Mr. Mueller was hoping Conor would use the same name for his password. So he came out here to see if he could find the password on our computer. I know it sounds kind of crazy..." Her voice trailed off and the kitchen was silent.

Mr. McCormick closed his eyes and rubbed the bridge of his nose. Finally he looked at Addie. "Your hunches might be good ones, but that's all they are. Hunches. I'm not about to accuse a respected teacher of anything without solid proof."

"I don't want to!" Addie exclaimed. "I don't really care if we prove whether or not Mr. Mueller is a...a 'pirate.' I just want to prove Conor isn't."

"How?"

"We can go with him to Mr. Beland's office, explain why he was there Saturday, and get his game from the vault. If Conor is guilty—if there isn't a game and he's stolen the disks—he won't want to go. But if he's not guilty, he'll jump at the chance."

Mr. McCormick regarded his daughter soberly. "I suppose it's worth a try. I told Mr. Beland I would talk to the boy. We'll go tomorrow after school if Conor agrees."

Addie excused herself and ran to the phone. She found the Davises' phone number and made the call. It was an awkward conversation at first. But when Conor realized Addie was on his side, he relaxed.

"Thanks a lot, Addie," he said warmly. "I'll be glad to have all this out in the open. All I ever wanted to do was find my game."

"I know," Addie said. "Can you go tomorrow after school?"

"Sure," Conor said. "See you then."

Addie came back to the table and sat down with a satisfied smile. "I knew—" The shrill ring of the telephone interrupted her, and she pushed her chair back to get up once more, but her father stopped her.

"Finish your supper," he said. "I'll answer it."

He went to the hall and picked up the phone. Addie dug into her fried chicken with zeal, keeping one ear tuned to the conversation in the next room.

"Hello?" her father said. "Well, hello . . . No, we just sat down, it's no problem . . . Yes, Addie mentioned that . . . Oh, I see . . . um . . ."

Mr. McCormick's end of the conversation deteriorated into a series of *um's* and *um-huh's*, and Addie grew frustrated trying to figure out what the conversation was about. She soon gave up and began telling her mother about the variety of people she had seen in the mall that day.

Finally her father began talking in complete sentences again, and Addie tuned back in.

"I understand . . . I'm glad you called. We were a little concerned about it . . . No, under the circumstances there's nothing else you could have done . . . of course . . . no, really, it's all right . . . Thanks for calling . . . um-huh . . . Goodbye."

Mr. McCormick hung up the phone, came back to the kitchen, and sat down heavily in his chair. He picked up his fork and began stirring his mashed potatoes, mixing them with the gravy until they were all brown and soupy.

Addie made a face. "That's pretty gross, Dad. Who was that on the phone?"

"Jim Mueller."

Addie's eyes grew wide, and she stopped chewing in mid-bite. "What did he want?"

"Well, kiddo, it seems you were right. Mr. Mueller was here this afternoon. He came out to the house to get the disk he loaned us on Saturday. He said he saw you at the mall and thought you and Mom would be home by the time he got out here. But of course you weren't, and the door was open, so he let himself in and got the disk from the drawer. It seems he promised to show the games to the computer science teacher at Loman at a faculty meeting tonight."

Mrs. McCormick was relieved. "Well, that explains our 'visitor,' doesn't it? That sounds like a logical explanation to me. He probably didn't *plan* to walk into our house. How was he to know I'd leave the door unlocked? And I certainly don't care if he came in to get the disk, do you?"

"No, but—"

Addie couldn't hold back her suspicions. "Why didn't he just use the originals he has at the high school?

Mr. McCormick shrugged. "I thought of that myself."

"And why did he open up the games on our computer?" Addie continued. "They're not the same as the games on the disk that he wanted."

"He didn't offer any explanation for that," said Mr. McCormick, "and I didn't ask."

"John!" Mrs. McCormick said reprovingly. "You're beginning to sound like Addie."

"Addie's beginning to make more sense," Mr. McCormick said grimly. He took a deep breath. "I guess we'll find out tomorrow, won't we?"

Epilogue

"Feet of Clay"

The next afternoon, Conor, Addie, and Mr. McCormick all sat in front of Mr. Beland's desk.

"Let me get this straight," the superintendent said. "You wrote the game Mr. Mueller was going to show to Addie's class?"

Conor nodded. "Mr. Mueller said it was one of the best he'd ever seen," the boy said proudly.

"And you found a copy of this game in the vault on Saturday?"

Conor blushed. "I'm sorry. I know it was wrong, but the door was open. I just had to look."

"There are other disks missing," Mr. Beland said. "At least two that I know of."

"I didn't take them," Conor insisted. "I didn't even take my game. I put it back."

Mr. Beland drummed his fingers on the desk and studied Conor carefully. There was a quiet knock at the door, and Mr. Mueller peered into the office.

"Mr. Mueller," the superintendent said. "Come right in. We've got some things to talk about."

Mr. Mueller stepped into the office and looked curiously from the McCormicks to Conor.

"Conor tells me he wrote a game in your computer science class—the game you were going to show the sixth-graders."

Mr. Mueller glanced briefly at Conor and gave a short nod.

"I thought there was only one copy of that game," Mr. Beland continued.

"I was wrong," Mr. Mueller said with some difficulty. "I happen to have another copy of it in my room."

"Could that be one of the disks I told you was missing from my vault?"

"It . . . could be," Mr. Mueller said. "I found several disks in my drawer this morning. I came to tell you I had them. I thought I'd signed them out. I guess I was wrong."

"I guess you were," Mr. Beland said dryly. "Why don't you bring Conor's game to the office? We'll give him a copy, since he won't be back at Heritage until next fall."

Mr. Mueller nodded and hurried from the room.

Mr. Beland and Addie's father talked quietly while they waited for Mr. Mueller. Conor simply sat and stared at the floor. When Mr. Mueller returned with the disk, Conor took it from him silently.

"It's really a very good game, Conor," Mr. Mueller said. "I'm sure you could sell it if you wanted to."

Conor gave his teacher a hard look. "Did you do anything to it?"

Mr. Mueller shook his head. "I couldn't even get into it. I never did figure out the password." He glanced quickly at the McCormicks and his face reddened.

Conor gave a satisfied nod, but he left the room without another word. Addie followed him, and Mr. McCormick stood to shake hands with Mr. Beland. As he closed the door, Addie heard Mr. Beland speak.

"You better sit down, Jim," he said. "I think we need to talk."

* * *

The ride home was very quiet. Conor stared out the window the whole time. Addie didn't feel there was anything she could say, so she wisely kept silent.

Mr. McCormick pulled into the Davises' drive and stopped the car. But Conor didn't make any effort to get out. Finally he spoke.

"He was going to steal my game." It wasn't a question, just a statement.

Mr. McCormick didn't try to make any excuses for the teacher. Instead he said, "Conor, have you ever heard the expression 'feet of clay'?"

Conor shrugged and nodded.

"We all have them. Mr. Mueller is no exception."

"He's a teacher!" The words practically exploded out of Conor. Then, more quietly, "I trusted him."

"And he failed you. People always will, Conor. You still have to forgive them."

"He didn't even apologize!"

Now it was Mr. McCormick's turn to shrug. "Doesn't matter. You're not responsible for what he does. You're responsible for how you react. If you hang onto this, you'll only hurt yourself."

"I don't think I can ever forget what he did," Conor said.

"It will take a long time," Mr. McCormick agreed. "In the meantime, try to learn from it."

"What do you mean?" Conor asked.

"Any one of us could make the mistakes Mr. Mueller made," the older man said. "Everybody has an area in their life that gives them trouble."

Addie spoke for the first time. "I'm too impulsive. I jump into things before I think."

Mr. McCormick grinned at his daughter. "And it gets you in trouble, doesn't it?"

Addie didn't bother to answer.

"If you're forced to face your problem area and suffer the consequences, you usually turn around and try to change."

"Repent," Conor said.

Mr. McCormick looked a little surprised, but he smiled. "Exactly. That's what 'repent' means. I don't think Mr. Mueller has ever had to face the consequences of his actions. He's probably gotten away with 'bending the rules' all his life. Maybe this experience will help him repent."

"Maybe." Conor didn't sound too hopeful. "Anyway, I'll think about what you said."

He stuck his hand out awkwardly, and Mr. McCormick shook it. "Thanks," the young boy said simply. "I could have been in big trouble without your help. I wish there was something I could do for you."

"Just keep tutoring my wife," Mr. McCormick laughed. "She still hasn't figured out how to change the margins on her word processing program."

Conor smiled. "I'll show her tomorrow," he promised. He opened the car door, but Addie grabbed his arm from the backseat before he could get out.

"Conor, wait," she said. "Can I ask you something?"

Conor nodded.

"I've always been curious. What's your game about?"

Conor was amazed. "You mean I've never told you?"

Addie shook her head.

"It's a history game that helps you develop thinking skills," Conor explained. "You get to choose a time in history when important things were happening, for instance, World War II. Your player is placed in the middle of a dangerous situation. In one of the scenarios, you're a Jewish woman and you find yourself on a train. But you don't know how you got there or where you're going.

"So you have to ask the computer questions to find out as much as you can about your situation. Then you have to decide the best way out of your problem. The decisions you make almost always change the course of history."

"Sounds good," Addie said. "What's it called?"

Conor grinned. *"Look Before You Leap."*

Addie couldn't help but laugh. "Sounds like my kind of game!"

About the Author

Leanne Lucas grew up reading mysteries by a creek near her childhood home in central Illinois. Secret visits to a nearby abandoned house later provided the inspiration for many of Addie's adventures. Leanne enjoys naming her characters after friends and family—Addie was named for a woman she worked with at the University of Illinois.

Leanne and her husband, David, own their own business and homeschool their son, Joshua. They reside in Homer, Illinois, where they share their home with Josh's grandma, four hermit crabs, and a cat named Star.

The Action Never Stops in
The Crista Chronicles
by Mark Littleton

Secrets of Moonlight Mountain

When an unexpected blizzard traps Crista on Moonlight Mountain with a young couple in need of a doctor, Crista must brave the storm and the dark to get her physician father. Will she make it in time?

Winter Thunder

A sudden change in Crista's new friend, Jeff, and the odd circumstances surrounding Mrs. Oldham's broken windows all point to Jeff as the culprit in the recent cabin break-ins. What is Jeff trying to hide? Will Crista be able to prove his innocence?

Robbers on Rock Road

When the clues fall into place regarding the true identity of the cabin-wreckers, Crista and her friends find themselves facing terrible danger! Can they stop the robbers on Rock Road before someone gets hurt?

Escape of the Grizzly

A grizzly is on the loose on Moonlight Mountain! Who will find the bear first—the sheriff's posse or the circus workers? Crista knows there isn't much time... the bear has to be found quickly. But where, and how? Doing some fast thinking, Crista comes up with a plan...

Find Adventure and Excitement in
The Maggie's World Series
by Eric Wiggin

Maggie: Life at The Elms

Maggie's father died at the Battle of Gettysburg, and the man her mother is going to marry has a son who Maggie just can't stand! She asks for permission to live with her Grandpa in the deep woods of northern Maine—at his special home, The Elms.

Little does Maggie know how much her life is about to change—all because of an overfriendly hound dog, a rude, sharp-tongued girl at a logging camp, clever kitchen thieves in the night, and surprising lessons about friendship and forgiveness.

Maggie's Homecoming

After two years in the deep woods with Grandpa, Maggie is eager to return home. She and her stepbrother, Jack, must learn to get along—and to everyone's amazement, they do!

Before she has a chance to settle into her new home, Maggie is caught in another adventure. One Saturday she and Jack decide to explore a long-abandoned farmhouse around the mountainside—only to find out the place isn't abandoned after all . . .